PENGUIN BOOKS

THE WORLD BETWEEN

D1102338

C016988583

Also by Sarah Ann Juckes

Outside

THE WORLD BETWEEN US

Sarah Ann Juckes

PENGUIN BOOKS

PENGUIN BOOKS

UK | USA | Canada | Ireland | Australia
India | New Zealand | South Africa

Penguin Books is part of the Penguin Random House group of companies
whose addresses can be found at global.penguinrandomhouse.com.

www.penguin.co.uk
www.puffin.co.uk
www.ladybird.co.uk

Penguin
Random House
UK

First published 2021

001

Text copyright © Sarah Ann Juckes, 2021

The moral right of the author has been asserted

Set in 10.75/15.5 pt Adobe Caslon Pro
Typeset by Jouve (UK), Milton Keynes
Printed and bound in Great Britain by Clays Ltd, Elcograf S.p.A.

The authorized representative in the EEA is Penguin Random House Ireland,
Morrison Chambers, 32 Nassau Street, Dublin D02 YH68

A CIP catalogue record for this book is available from the British Library

ISBN: 978-0-241-46207-2

All correspondence to:
Penguin Books
Penguin Random House Children's
One Embassy Gardens, 8 Viaduct Gardens
London SW11 7BW

For Ryan

Welcome back to Stream Cast, Alice

Users online:

WesleyCycles67
Online for:
3 mins

tokyo--drifter
Online for:
4 hours

Users offline:

destroy_roy
Last online:
14 hours

1mp0ssibledream
Last online:
1 day

daddycool-007
Last online:
50 days

Connect to a channel to start watching.

Connecting to **WesleyCycles67** . . .

1

WesleyCycles67

And now I am strapped to the chest of a middle-aged man called Wesley as he straps his feet on to the pedals of his bike.

It's still dark, but I can just about see his hand as he sets his watch to zero and pushes off.

His little street with the Monopoly houses curves round to a main road and we don't have to stop and wait for the traffic today – we just cycle right into it and we're riding – faster and faster – as the street lamps putter out behind us and the world is swallowed by darkness. Flashlight cars overtake us, and I can see glimpses of scarecrows in the fields. Eyes peering from bushes.

He checks his watch and cycles faster. Today we could beat his commute record. This morning could go down in history.

The road dips and everything blurs, but still we keep pedalling. His legs are going so fast I'm not sure if he'll be able to keep up with them, but he does. And, when the road levels, we overtake the traffic-stuck cars that passed us before, and we glance through their windows to see the drivers' looks of surprise – a quick flash – before we're gone again.

The sun raises an eyebrow above the horizon and the lights from the cars stretch into neon lines, criss-crossing lanes like a stampede of metal, and we're in the thick of it, zigzagging between bumpers, beating amber traffic lights, mounting pavements and jumping down kerbs to avoid belly-lit bollards and parked cars.

And we can see the finish line now – the bell tower jutting into the clouds from the middle of the school Wesley works at. And we have sixty seconds and one set of traffic lights to go through. They're on red, but the way is clear so we don't slow down.

And then.

Very much from nowhere.

A car.

And we brake and we brake and we brake.

And I'm screaming, because we're going too fast and the car wasn't there a moment ago and now it is.

I listen as Wesley's heart leaps out of its cage as the rest of him

stops.

Carbon fibre fractures. The camera that he had strapped to his chest. Shatters.

WesleyCycles67 is no longer streaming.
Please choose another channel.

2

Alice

Two weeks ago, I died.

But I'm trying not to think about that, as today is a burst of brand new. The sun shining from under my closed curtains is turning Manta's fish tank into rainbows, and Mum is absent-mindedly singing one of her old show tunes downstairs while she dishes up my breakfast and sorts out my meds.

I smile at her as she comes into my room, and the singing stops. 'Oh, sorry, sweetheart, I hope I didn't wake you.'

'That's okay,' I say. 'You can keep singing.'

But she doesn't. She's all tiptoes and hushed tones now as she opens the curtains and sets the bed to snail speed. And the room's much too quiet for the angry buzzing of the bed motor slowly lifting me up, so I slide on my headphones and disappear into violins and flutes. I lie back and listen, trying to remember what it felt like to be cycling through fields with Wesley at weekends, chasing sheep while looking out at a sea of green cut against an almost perfect line of blue sky.

And then that car comes out of nowhere and everything stops again.

By the time I'm upright, I'm already out of breath.

Mum slides off my headphones. 'How many spoons are we starting with today?'

'Ten, I think,' I say, although I said that yesterday and I was spent by eight.

Sitting up in bed = 1 spoon

Spoons are units of energy. When you're trapped in bed by a chronic Illness, like I am, there are only so many units to go around. You might have an endless cutlery drawer full of spoons, but these days mine are all in a wobbly pot.

One unit of energy = 1 spoon

We started talking in spoons after we read a blog by Christine Miserandino, who used them as a metaphor for energy loss. Somehow, they've found their way into our everyday, now.

When you wake up with only ten spoons, you need to make every single one count.

Mum passes me my breakfast and I try to look happy about having smoked salmon again, for the fifth day in a row.

'I know.' She sighs at my strained smile. 'It's your dad's fault. They had an offer on it and he's packed the fridge full of the bloody stuff. We'll all be eating it for the next year.'

Dad sticks his head round the door. 'It was two-for-one, though. You never see that on salmon.'

Mum rolls her eyes and mutters, 'Thinks we have money to burn, that man.'

The salmon is nice. So are the eggs. But I can't shake the image of that car racing towards us and swallowing seems to take up more spoons than it should.

Eating breakfast = 2 spoons

Dad sneaks in as Mum disappears, and sits on the edge of my bed.

'How's tricks, kiddo?'

I smile, but keep my eyes on the skirting board. 'Oh, I'm fine.'

He's still looking at me and I can tell that smiles and pleasantries aren't going to cut it today. So I pull my eyes over to his and try to keep them steady. 'How was the funeral?'

'Oh, you know – typical funeral really. A barrel of laughs.'

I wouldn't know. I've never been to a funeral. But the dark circles under his eyes tell me that they might not be a laughing matter.

'I recorded it for you.'

He picks up my plate and starts eating my leftovers like it's nothing.

I swallow. 'Oh?'

'Yup. Took a camera in specially. Sat at the back – although you'd think I'd brought in a fricking clown from the dirty looks I was getting. You're welcome, by the way.'

I pick at my nails. 'That's okay. Thank you, but I don't need to watch it.'

Forgetting is a far more difficult task at a funeral.

He stops eating. 'Alice. This is Wesley we're talking about. I know you never met him in real life, but you were with the bloke every morning on that bike. You were with him when he died, for crying out –'

'Yes, okay!' I say, panic jumping up my throat.

7

Dad looks at me. Hard. I take a breath.

'Okay,' I say. 'I'll watch it. Thank you.'

Dad pats my hand. 'Let's get you ready, then, and we'll pop it on.'

Getting ready. Walking unsteadily to the en suite. Brushing my hair. Brushing my teeth. Having a wash. Staring at myself in the mirror for a good long time and wondering if I'd look less like my Black Moor goldfish if I bleached my hair blonde, or lost the fringe.

Getting ready = 5 spoons

I'm at eight spoons already and it isn't even ten o'clock, so Dad helps me back from the en suite and into the black dress I wore for my sixteenth birthday last month. I climb into bed, panting like I've been cycling up a hill.

The footage Dad took at the funeral is set up on the laptop, ready to go.

I want to complain. Make up an excuse. Tell him that I don't need to watch this after all, thank you. That I'm happy in my room, keeping my mind on meadows and music and goldfish.

But there aren't enough spoons left to protest.

Dad leans over and presses play.

3

daddycool-007

And now I am at a funeral with my dad.

We're sitting at the very back, but he's holding me up high enough so that I can see over the heads. There are probably around a hundred people in front of us, all sitting in rows like black crows on telephone wires.

And there's Wesley. The one inside the coffin with the shards of the camera still wedged inside his chest.

That camera had been my Christmas present last year. Dad gave it to me because I'd started to see the walls and he wanted to give me a window. At first, he would just go on adventures with it strapped to his chest, filming things for me to watch later. But then he discovered Stream Cast – a streaming site with a private channel open only to me, where I could log on any time through my laptop and watch the world Living live. And there was something magical about that.

Wesley was my first streamer. He worked with Mum at the school down the road, and she convinced him to live-stream his commute in the morning. Then Dad got my cousin Roy involved, who was born the day after me and plays a lot of computer games. And Dad met a friend at tae kwon do who takes me training, and my old babysitter, Hana, streams all the way from Tokyo, where she lives now.

But Wesley was always my favourite. When I was with him on his bike, it was like I'd banished the Illness and I was Living fast. I saw pheasants bursting out from bushes like feathered rainbows, and rabbit tails bouncing like ping-pong balls into burrows. I saw crops reaching up and flaming, until whole fields were ablaze with yellow fire. I saw puddles turn into rivers turn into wide lakes, the water as many different colours as the sky.

I did my very best Living with Wesley, so it does feel like this is my funeral somehow, too.

If this were my funeral, though, I suppose Dad wouldn't be sitting at the back, the camera he's holding up receiving angry stares.

A man who I think is a priest stands up at the front and starts talking. I can't hear what he's saying because we're too far away, but it's probably about how Wesley Lived his life by the clock and how time does seem to have stopped now he's no longer Living.

If he were talking about me, it'd probably be about what I was like before the Illness came and took me, because people do seem to find that easier to remember. He'd be talking about me as if I died at ten, when I went on adventures with Dad, won that trophy for breaststroke, ate aniseed balls by the bag, listened to music at full blast and wanted nothing more than to be a marine biologist one day.

He wouldn't be talking about me after the Illness. When I caught some silly virus going round at school and then didn't seem to get better while everybody else did. He wouldn't be speaking about the girl who slowly stopped being able to go to school. Then outside. Then leave her bed. He wouldn't mention the Illness and how no one knew quite what it was, even after all those years, and all those tests, and all those Google symptom searches. If I'm honest, I wouldn't blame him for that. Who wants to hear about a girl who's exhausted after having a wash?

The thing most people don't understand, though, is that I don't have to Live inside these four walls. I don't have to be trapped inside my body. I can be strapped to the chest of brilliant people and I can watch them Live lives that could perhaps be my own, and that's a thing of wonder.

That is, until one of them dies.

The priest stands aside and a woman I think is Wesley's wife gets up and I use my last spoons to lean over and slam the laptop closed.

Welcome back to Stream Cast, Alice

Users online:

destroy_roy
Online for:
57 mins

Users offline:

1mp0ssibledream
Last online:
4 hours

tokyo--drifter
Last online:
3 days

WesleyCycles67
Last online:
18 days

daddycool-007
Last online:
68 days

Connect to a channel to start watching.

Connecting to **destroy_roy** . . .

4

destroy_roy

And now I am balanced on the desk of my sixteen-year-old cousin Roy as he hammers at his keyboard like he's playing some ferocious piano.

There's no music that I can hear, though. Instead, I watch his screen as he stalks through an apocalyptic landscape, his hands clutching a gun as he runs towards a derelict building.

I don't recognize this game. Usually Roy streams himself playing games that involve building up whole worlds from nothing. And even though he never takes the camera outside, there's something brilliant about watching him breathe life into building blocks.

This game is different, though. His fingers are white on the keyboard. He pulls open the door to the building and crouches under an empty window, wrapping bandages round his computerized hands.

And then I hear the popping. Far away at first and then louder and louder. And I want to warn him, but he can't hear me and he probably doesn't even know I'm here with him, because that's not how Stream Cast works. It's not a two-way conversation. I just watch and shout into silence.

He reacts too late. His fighter stands up at the window as we see the van racing towards him, killers wearing tin helmets hanging out of the windows and speeding his way .

Pop-pop-pop-pop.

And the bullets hit him and hit him and the screen splashes red and the health bar drains to nothing and Roy is shouting in a way I've never heard him shout before and –

You have disconnected from this stream.

5

Alice

I throw the laptop down and grip the sides of my bed and, of course, Mum sees.

She hurries forward. I try to smile as if nothing's wrong, but my breathing's giving me away. She pinches each of my wrists between her forefinger and thumb.

'Nice steady breaths,' she says.

I close my eyes. Take myself away to another place for a moment, where I'm suspended in a whole ocean of multicoloured life.

I am safe. I am happy. I am alive.

I think it until I start feeling that it's true. The bad thoughts tie themselves into nice little bows and I fold them neatly in a drawer at the very back of my mind.

I open my eyes and smile at Mum as she searches my face for any wisps the thoughts left behind.

'Perhaps you should give Stream Cast a rest. Just for a while.'

I grab her hands. 'No! I'm fine, honestly. I was just being silly.'

Mum sighs. 'You can talk to me, you know. About Wesley. About anything.'

'I know.' I smile and try to shake Wesley's name away before it sticks. 'And I was going to talk to you, actually. About maybe getting me a new streamer. Someone who doesn't play shooting games, or fights, or walks round a busy city. Someone who just does normal, everyday things that I might do.'

Mum slides her hands away and picks up the blanket that slipped off the bed when I was trying to get away from the bullets. 'I'll think about it. But, Alice – think about what I said, too. I'm here if you want to talk.'

She puts the blanket back on my bed and irons out all the crinkles with her arm, and it feels as if she's doing the same to my brain – smoothing out all the thoughts of cars crashing into bikes, and soldiers being gunned down.

I nod and hope she can't tell how fast my heart is beating. Because – as much as I know that she'd do anything for me – I can't keep asking her to hold everything. Like how my chest is hurting today, or that the pain in my knees is back. I can see all that worry weighing her down and drawing lines on her face that shouldn't be there yet.

So I distract myself by focusing on all the wonderful things there are in the world, like how I'm back to twelve spoons today. And that means that when she leaves, and my phone starts to buzz like a bee trapped inside a window, I can lift myself slowly out and round my bed to answer it.

Walking round my bed = 2 spoons

I blink the black spots out of my eyes and remember to breathe as I walk with one hand on my bedframe, just in case. My phone's next to Manta's fish tank and he swims down to the bottom to see who it is.

It's Cecelia. Her face beams out at me from the screen mid-laugh.

I pick the phone up. 'Hello, you.'

'Oh my God, are you running, too? You sound like you've been running. I'm running round the park at the moment with all these people, Al. It's crazy – there are, like, a hundred people here, all running, and I just saw them and thought, hey, why not join them? I'm wearing sandals and am so sweaty in my jeans.'

She laughs and pants, and I laugh and pant, and I sit down on the bed and remind myself again to breathe.

Standing up = 1 spoon

'I've been . . . gaming. And now I'm visiting Manta.'

'You and that fish,' she says, and I can hear the thump of her legs on the ground, and the phone jumping at her face, and her lungs breathing the outside air, and it's wonderful.

Manta blows a bubble and I open the tub of food next to his tank and sprinkle a few flakes in. He picks off the bits at the surface before twirling to catch the ones falling like snow.

Feeding Manta = 1 spoon

'How old is that fish now, anyway? Do fish even live that long?'

'Yes!' I say. 'He's only six – they can live much longer than that.'

'Jeez,' she says, starting to gasp a bit now. 'You got him when you stopped school, didn't you? God, I can't believe that's been six years already. We're getting so old.'

I swallow and sit a bit further back on the bed. 'Tell me what you see.'

Cecelia laughs. 'Sweaty people. And running shoes, which I should definitely be wearing.'

I close my eyes as she lists the other things she can see and try to imagine me running next to her, although it's hard, because I never did do much running back when I could. I was too busy swimming instead – every day after school. Being in the water felt like coming home – as though I was born with gills and every moment of my life on land was me holding my breath. I used to pretend that I was freediving through mangroves and watching fish dart between tree roots. And I'd dream about one day disappearing somewhere far away, where the water is a window that you can push your hands right through.

'Come join me, Al,' Cecelia says, like she's reading my mind through the phone.

I shake my head, but I make myself stand up, my legs shivering a bit and my hand holding the wall for support. I walk, though, forward towards the bedroom door and out on to the landing, where I can see into my old box bedroom that now belongs to Mum and Dad, and the family bathroom I no longer use. And I can see the stairs tumbling down to the floor below.

'Come join me,' she says again.

And I think about what it would be like to walk down them, slip on a pair of sandals and go running with strangers, just because I could.

I miss a breath.

The phone drops from my hand and I watch Cecelia's face on the screen as it hits each step with a

Thud.

Thud.

Thud.

Standing on the landing = 2 spoons

Mum comes out of her room and catches me just in time. 'Alice! Not near the stairs!'

I gulp big glugs of air as she helps me back into bed.

No, not near the stairs. I still have the bruise from where I fainted walking to the en suite last week and it would be so much worse to fall all that way, even if I would get to see the other rooms downstairs, even for just a moment.

I get my breath back and watch Manta in his four-walled tank over her shoulder, dark like a shadow until the light hits him just right and he shines gold. And as Mum makes the bed go back down again, I tell her that Manta and I are the same. That my body may be stuck inside this bedroom-tank, but I'm free to shine a light wherever I please. The world is packed full of beautiful things with hidden gold, if only you look at them in

    the
           right
                 light
                       and

What was I saying?
I'm sorry, I seem to have lost . . .
No, no, I'm not tired.
It's my body.
It's
        stopped.

6

Alice

And now I am dreaming.

I'm floating in an endless ocean and all around me is a deep royal blue. And I feel weightless. Calm. Like I'm moving towards something, caught on an invisible tide that's tunnelling under the waves and taking me somewhere.

But then I twirl. And below me I see rocks jutting out of the seabed. Rocks with shards of glass and splinters of carbon fibre glittering between them.

I struggle. I gulp water and the tide spins me round and I lose all sense of up and down. And suddenly the seabed is the sky and above me is Mum. Dad. Cecelia. All paddling at the top, their legs like sunbeams that can't reach down to me in the dark.

I stretch my fingers out to them. I kick with every ounce of energy I have.

But still. I sink.

7

Alice

Sometimes the Illness will take spoons faster than I can count and it'll take Me along with my body.

That's the worst part. I can cope well enough with my limbs breaking down now, as if they're powered by cheap batteries with an hour's life in them. But when it takes my mind I lose all sense of who I am. My 'Me'. It'll take an hour to type a short text message or remember the name of my own goldfish. It feels like being trapped on a raft in the middle of an ocean of brain fog, just floating into nothing.

'Ugh, I'm going to be late again,' Mum says as she rushes to get ready for work. 'Are you going to be okay on your own today, Alice?'

'Yes, of course,' I say, picking up my laptop. 'I'm back to a full set of spoons now.'

But as she kisses me goodbye, looks at her watch and swears, I wonder if that's entirely true.

Welcome back to Stream Cast, Alice

Users online:

tokyo--drifter
Online for:
16 mins

Users offline:

1mp0ssibledream	**destroy_roy**	**WesleyCycles67**
Last online:	Last online:	Last online:
4 hours	4 days	22 days

daddycool-007
Last online:
72 days

Connect to a channel to start watching.

Hana is online. And, even though I feel a slight pang above my eye, I click to connect and disappear.

Connecting to **tokyo--drifter** . . .

8

tokyo--drifter

And now I am being held on a selfie stick as I watch my old babysitter, Hana, wander round wide pedestrian streets with whole forests of buildings either side.

She has the camera turned to face her, which is something she always does and I don't know why. It makes it impossible to believe that I'm walking round Tokyo with her. Why would I ever walk backwards?

Her hair is in pigtails and she's smiling at everyone she walks past, but I try to see beyond her face to the city behind her.

Tokyo is buildings and glass-fronted arcades and lights that flash like a Christmas tree. There are people everywhere, holding hands and cameras, and pointing at things higher than I can see.

She swings the selfie stick round and I feel like I'm being helicoptered. She eventually sits on something I think is a bench, watching something I can't see behind the camera. Some music starts up and someone's singing, and I keep expecting her to turn the camera towards the action. Instead, I watch her watch whatever it is with her mouth open.

'Turn the camera round,' I say out loud, but of course she can't hear me. The streamers never can.

I'm thinking about disconnecting when I catch the shopfront screen behind her. It was advertising a soft drink, but now it's turned into what looks like a giant fish tank – as if it isn't a screen at all, but a portal into a world within a world.

The screen shows the sea as if I'm sitting on the seabed, not my own bed, or even a bench in the middle of Tokyo. Thousands of multicoloured fish dart about, flitting between long-fingered coral and short-fingered divers. Turtles stroke their way over my head and whales blast out fountains at the top.

And I'm reminded that the sea is filled with Living. From tiny green specks of life all the way to its biggest monsters. It's a place to float. To be everything and nothing and everyone and no one. Where there are no spoons to be taken – just silence. Just light.

I breathe it in and it's like the whole world seems to stop, just for one moment.

And then the band Hana was watching finishes and she uses both hands to clap, dissolving the stream into bubbles.

You have disconnected from this stream.

9

Alice

I close my laptop. The house is silent with Mum and Dad at work. There's just the sound of my breaths, the light buzzing of Manta's tank and the breeze from the open window making my curtains flutter against the window sill.

And outside, in the distance, I see the bell tower. Wesley's own finish line and the last thing he saw before –

I shake my head. It used to be nice to have the window open and see, just one street away, the school where Cecelia studies and Mum works as a careers advisor, helping lost students navigate their way through life after lessons.

Before the Illness got me, Mum was a singer. She toured in a Spice Girls cover band as Posh Spice – which Dad and I always found ironic, seeing as we've both witnessed her eat crumbs from her bra. But onstage she was a star. And I used to love watching her perform, holding her microphone out to the crowd and getting the whole room dancing.

These days, she keeps her music low and the singing to downstairs, where the sound can't reach me and take spoons. And, instead of a microphone, she holds meetings about other people's dreams.

I watch Mum putting her life on pause to look after me and I feel the guilt like a thousand tonnes of water on my bones. It makes me feel heavy, and the walls of my room a little smaller, and the empty-house silence almost –

I take a deep breath and open my laptop again. My mouse hovers over the Stream Cast icon on my desktop.

Welcome back to Stream Cast, Alice

Users online:

Rowan
Online for:
2 minutes

tokyo--drifter
Online for:
4 hours

Users offline:

1mp0ssibledream
Last online:
4 days

destroy_roy
Last online:
7 hours

WesleyCycles67
Last online:
22 days

daddycool-007
Last online: 72 days

Connect to a channel to start watching.

My blood seems to freeze mid-pump.

Rowan. Online for two minutes.

It's a new streamer. And the thumbnail by their name is dark, like they might be existing at the bottom of a black sea, too.

My heart kick-starts again and now I'm shaking, because I have a new window. A window that could be a world apart from bad things or lives that could be lost at any moment. A window that's open and ready for me to climb through and leave my body and all its broken parts behind.

I rub the growing pain just above my eye. I click.

And I climb through.

Connecting to **Rowan** . . .

10

Rowan

And now I am strapped to the chest of a person I don't know as they walk through what I think is a long tunnel.

There's light up ahead, and the view rocks from side to side as they walk unsteadily. I can hear footsteps echoing and I hold my breath like I used to do when I drove through tunnels with Dad, back before the Illness. And I can almost hear the sound boomeranging back and pushing me – making me feel as if I might never take a breath again – as yellow strip lights strobe above us in time to my heartbeat. And we're racing – racing towards the finish line, where there's a whole new life waiting, with crisp, fresh air. But we're not going fast enough and the thrill of perhaps not being able to make it charges through my bones.

But the light is getting closer now, flaring up on the camera as the lens adjusts. And I want us to keep walking into that light. Into that new life where there's no such thing as shadow.

But instead the new streamer stops. Turns. And looks at the tunnel wall.

I let out my breath.

Why are we looking at the tunnel wall when there's a whole new world waiting in the light? It's just a wall. Someone has even graffitied over the concrete cracks with criss-cross signs and symbols, like a giant game of noughts and crosses. I want us to turn and keep walking towards the light, to where the Living is done. But we don't move. We just keep staring.

My stomach sinks. This was supposed to be a new window, but now I'm lumbered with someone who likes to look at walls instead of doing any of the things I'd do if my body worked as it did before. Like swim to impossible places and see colour burst out of the blue.

But then I look. Really look. And, as I'm staring, I see the lines drawn on the wall are criss-crossing into something bigger. Bigger than me and even the wall itself. The tiny scratches of colour zigzag into each other to make a line. To make an eye. To make eight legs with hundreds of tiny suckers on each one.

The new streamer steps back and suddenly I see that the drawing is of a giant rainbow squid, bursting out of the tunnel wall as if it has dipped its legs in a thousand pots of paint and thrashed itself into being. The flickering strip lights make it seem like it's breathing, writhing on the concrete, getting ready to wrap itself round the heart of the world and squeeze.

As we stand there, a man in a suit pushes past, his eyes glued to his phone, head down. Not seeing. But we see.

And I wonder how many other things a Living person will miss because they're busy racing to their next meeting, when there are all sorts of wonders, like this one, hiding in the cracks.

Finally, we turn and walk out of the tunnel and I'm almost sad to say goodbye to the kraken taking down the concrete, as the new light washes out the picture for a moment. But then it clears, and I see a path snaking round a children's playground.

The new streamer walks with their hands in their pockets, or so I think, and it makes the world tilt left and right as they raise each foot and put it down. We follow the path until it spits us out on a spongey kind of tarmac, which I imagine feels like standing in the middle of a black birthday cake.

It's a grey kind of day, but children in blue sweaters are rocketing from all directions to the playground, screaming as they jump on the back of swings, and cling on for dear life as the roundabouts turn them into bubblegum ice-cream swirls.

I would have thought the new streamer would have been put off by all these children, but whoever it is doesn't seem to mind. Instead, they climb the steps to the castle-themed climbing frame two at a time, and I see hands as they grab hold of rusted handles and pull us up – fingers long and strong like spider crabs.

They walk with their knees and head bent as they squeeze into the tower at the top – a slide lolling out of one window and a pole shooting down from another.

I'm wondering which one they're going to choose to go down. I hope it's the slide first and then the pole, because I can just about remember that stomach flip when you give your body over to gravity and simply fall. But instead they sit down – black sneakers with holes in the tops kicking up in front of them, and jeans gathered at the ankles covering legs that don't mind being used.

I don't think they're a teacher from the school again like Wes–
I shake my head.

I think this streamer's young. But seeing as they have to put their feet up on the wall to fit inside the make-believe children's castle, they're not a kid any more.

And then I see it. Their feet are in the way, but behind them I see a drawing – by the same artist as the kraken, I'm sure of it. It's the same style: hundreds of tiny lines, each one a different colour, twisting round each other to make scales, which make a tail, which makes a rather haunted-looking mermaid. Her tail wraps round the window to the slide as her arms clutch the frame of the window to the pole as if she, too, can't decide which one to launch herself out of first.

Her hair is nothing like the mermaid from the Disney film – it's every shade of blue the sea has, with strands wrapped in green weeds and purple shells. She's naked on top, but she wears an expression like she thinks there are more pressing things going on in the world than who sees her boobs.

I follow her sunset eyes burning down out of the window she's holding. From here, you can see for miles and miles – across a field where some boys are playing football, using their T-shirts as goalposts – across a road with a bakery and a shop selling sherbets – across rows of houses and buildings and lamp posts – all the way to a vast expanse of blue.

'The sea!' I gasp.

I'm already imagining myself diving right into it, so when the new streamer opens their mouth it almost sounds like it's coming from somewhere up on the surface.

'Huh –
I don't even notice the sea from here usually.
Weird.'

I stop.

And then I swallow a breath all at once and it scrambles like ice water in my lungs and I'm panicking, because they –

They heard me. And they just *spoke*. To *me*.

You have disconnected from this stream.

11

Alice

I slam the laptop closed and throw it on the floor, which makes a colossal thump. Just like my heart is doing. Again and again.

I sink down my pillow and kick up my duvet, where the air is too warm to come into my lungs that fast and I can breathe. Breathe.

And think.

The new streamer. They heard me speak. They must have done, because they answered me, even though it was a silly answer. Who lives by the sea and doesn't see it?

But the thing that's whirring through my head, and making that oh-so-familiar pain jam like a knife into the bone above my right eye, is that I don't talk to the streamers. Not to Wes–, not to any of them. I watch them Live their lives and pretend that I don't even have a mouth to speak out of. That I have left the Illness. The need to count spoons. This bed.

I push my fingers into my forehead to try and stop the migraine. If I could only just think for a moment more, I might be able to get my head round it.

The brain fog descends and all my thoughts peel away. I reach out my fingers and try to catch the letters as my words

d i s a p p e a r.

Then – like a lighthouse through the mist –

'All right, kiddo, just swallow this for me and you can rest, okay?'

Pill. It will stop the pain, but it will also stop Me.

Water.

Swallow.

'The bucket's here if you need it, right side of the bed.'

Beard kiss. Right where the pain is throbbing.

'Thanks, Dad,' I whisper.

And I am not Alice. I am not the new streamer. I am not even Me.

I am a migraine.

12

Alice

Having a migraine = 12 spoons

I hate migraines. They come like knives in the night to strike you down, leaving oil-spill darkness and a full-up bucket by the side of the bed.

Even with the pill dulling the edges, migraines will take enough spoons for two or three days, so it's all you can do just to stay awake and try to remember to eat and drink.

I'm starting to feel a bit more like Me again today, though, so when Mum calls up to say Cecelia has popped in for breakfast before school I don't tell her she can't come up.

'What's with all the salmon in your fridge?' Cecelia asks, tumbling into the room with a Pop-Tart and doing a running jump on to the bed beside me.

She hugs me tight and I pat her arm. 'Oh, you know – Dad.'

She offers me a bite of her Pop-Tart and I pull a face until she takes it away again.

'Climbing was cancelled this morning, can you believe it? They didn't even text anyone, so we all got up at six for absolutely no reason. Six! I tell you, Al, it's a good job I have you across the street, or I'd still just be waiting outside school for the doors to open, like the rest of those losers. What are we watching?'

I try to close the lid on my laptop, but she holds it open. I was watching _1mp0ssibledream_ stream – my dad's old tae kwon do buddy. I was watching his fists *punch-punch-punch* into a brightly coloured bag, and the room spin as he swept his leg back to kick it.

'Is this one of your weird streamers again? Honestly, you'll be watching one day and they'll suddenly just flop their wrinkly old-man penis out, and that's something you'll never be able to unsee, Al. Think about it.'

I laugh and push the laptop to the end of the bed. 'They're not like that!'

She takes another bite of her Pop-Tart. 'Weird old men with cameras are always like that.'

'Well,' I say, sitting up higher, 'they're not all old. Roy streams and he's our age.'

She rolls her eyes. 'Your cousin? That proves nothing. I remember him hiding all afternoon in the cupboard-under-your-stairs at your ninth birthday party, pretending to be Harry Potter, when there was a mother-fudging bouncy castle outside.' She shakes her head so her box braids flick into my face. 'He's as bad as you with this hermit stuff.'

I feel myself blush and suddenly I can see the wallpaper uncurling in the corner of my room, the empty pill packets littering the desk.

'It's useful to watch tae kwon do streams, anyway,' I say quickly. 'It helps me – it helps me perfect my kicks.'

I mime a fake tae kwon do kick into her shin.

Lying about doing tae kwon do = 2 spoons

'Jesus, yeah, you do need the practice,' she says, nudging me.

She finishes her Pop-Tart and talks about her friends at school – how they all want to start a bouldering club, with her as president.

And these are people who used to be my friends, too. Until they got a bit bored that I wasn't getting any better and stopped visiting. And Cecelia may say some silly things, but she's there for me. She remembers that I'm here and brings the outside here in a whirlwind that sweeps me into another life, if only for a moment.

'I am the best at bouldering, though. Watch,' she says.

She pushes her feet under the side of my mattress, hanging off the bedframe like a monkey, before trying and failing to leap across to my desk. She slams into the floor and rattles the water in Manta's tank.

I laugh so hard, my sides ache. And she rolls on the floor, clutching her sides, too, a swirl of purple highlights and chipped glitter nail polish and rainbow bangles on her arms.

'Oh my God, I think I ruptured something. Why do they make floors so hard?' she moans.

She reaches a hand up to me and I take it.

'That's a shame,' I say. 'You're just going to have to stay here on my carpet forever now.'

And I hope she can't see how tightly I'm holding on.

Mum comes in and raises an eyebrow. 'Not that I want to stop you putting a hole in the ceiling, but aren't you going to be late for crossing duty, Cecelia?'

Cecelia jumps up and digs her phone out of her pocket to look at the time. 'Oh shit, I forgot it was my turn!' She pats my foot in a sort of goodbye as she dashes out of the door, taking all the air with it, and I listen as she thuds downstairs and into her shoes and out of the door all over again. Not pausing to look at the rooms down there. Not stopping to take in all the things that you can never be sure you'll see again. Not pausing to stop. And see.

Mum shakes her head and then claps her hands together. 'Come on, then, you. Bath – before I have to run off to school, too.'

And, just like that, my whirlwind life has blown away and I'm back to being bedbound all over again.

Having a bath = 5 spoons

Cecelia's visit has left me with just a couple of spoons to last the day, so Mum helps me into the bath and runs the water.

I used to get embarrassed about her seeing me naked, but, just like the mermaid in the playground, there are perhaps more pressing things to worry about than whether it's okay for your mum to see your boobs.

She starts humming an old Spice Girls' song, and I want to listen to her. But it's a bit loud and echoey in the bathroom right now, so I have to ask her to stop. We sit in silence instead as she shampoos my hair.

The silence feels thick now, like it's swirling around with the steam from the water. It always feels this way after Cecelia visits. They're some of the only times I ever really let myself lose a spoon to talking. Of course, I chat to Mum and Dad.

And Manta, although he's yet to say a word back. And there are doctors and nurses and physiotherapists. But none of those conversations are really Me.

And even with Cecelia I end up lying. Not a lot. Just enough to hide the worst of the Illness from her. Just enough so that she doesn't stop visiting like the others did. Just enough to keep her coming back.

Perhaps that's why I freaked out when I accidentally spoke to the new streamer. I'm out of practice. Which is a shame, because there was everyone else, rushing about their day with their heads down, always wanting to get to where they were going faster – more efficiently. Just like . . . other people I know. Knew.

But this new streamer wasn't like that. I can tell they aren't Ill like me, because they're able to walk through tunnels and climb into castles, and I can't even keep my arms up to wash under them right now. But it was like wherever they were going had suddenly become not as important as where they were right then.

The same as it is with me.

And they saw things. Beautiful things. Things that someone else might tut at or paint over or rush by and not even see at all. And it almost makes me want to stop watching and start Living with them.

I look at Mum. 'You found me a new streamer.'

She pulls out the plug in the bath and the bubbles glug down. 'You saw him, then.'

I don't say anything back. I just let the water empty around me. She puts her elbows on the side of the bath and looks at me over her clasped hands.

'He was one of Wesley's art students, you know.'

My heart flutters at the name, but I try to keep my face neutral.

'The day before he died, Wesley left me a list of "lost" premium students he thought needed an extra push. I found it on my desk last week, and this boy was at the top. Wesley thought he could really be something special apparently.' She shrugs, like she doesn't quite believe it.

'What kind of "special"?' I ask slowly.

'The note didn't say. Something arty, I suppose. But, anyway, I thought you could help the kid find his purpose again. Be my spy on the inside.' She winks.

And I'm suddenly not sure how I feel, being a spy. Looking through someone's eyes that knew the eyes that have now closed forever. But then there's something else inside me that wants to know. Wants to be helpful to Mum, who's gone to the trouble of setting all this up for me. Wants to Live with the boy who stops, and sees, and could be something special.

'Okay.' I nod. 'I'll help.'

Welcome back to Stream Cast, Alice

Users online:

Rowan
Online for:
2 hours

1mp0ssibledream
Online for:
3 hours

Users offline:

tokyo--drifter
Last online:
12 hours

destroy_roy
Last online:
2 days

WesleyCycles67
Last online:
28 days

daddycool-007
Last online: 78 days

Connect to a channel to start watching.

Connecting to **Rowan** . . .

13

Rowan

And now I am strapped to the chest of the new streamer as he sits on a bench facing the gates of my old primary school. And I'm not here to be Me or him, but in between and both.

> *I feel like a bit of a prick wearing this camera strap.*
> *The elastic*
> *S T R E T C H E S*
> *into my sides.*
> *I bet I look like a right ham.*

And I remember. The green gates, tall like old trees. The boxy classrooms with blue-sweatered children in them. The playground painted with giant pencils. All in the shadow of the bell tower that was the last thing Wesley saw before he –

> *My phone gasps.*
> *'You're back, then?'*

I can't breathe. My silence just hangs there as he lifts an arm to his face, so all I can see for a moment is elbow.

I stuff my thumb into my eye.
'I screwed this up, didn't I?
That bloody careers lady
is gonna murder me.'

I manage to let out a croak this time. The idea of Mum murdering anyone is ridiculous.

'Listen.
Don't tell her I fucked this up,
will you?'
The new phone she gave me to do this
is way better than my old one.
It actually works, for one.

The F-word does something to jump-start me. 'There's no need to swear.'
 If Mum heard that, she really might murder him.
 He laughs.

'Sorry – Grandma.'
There are loads of old people around the school today.
To them, it probably looks like
I'm laughing at nothing. The bloke waiting next to me gives
me the side-eye.

Some of the children in the window of the classroom closest to us get up all at once and start packing books into folders.

'How am I speaking to you?' I say. 'I don't usually . . . streamers can't usually hear me.'

I eye the bloke back.
'It's a phone. Speaking's what it's for.
That and games.'
I've already downloaded Jonah's favourite.
Some stupid thing with birds
killing pigs.
What an education I'm providing him with.

No one else ever streamed from their phone, I don't think. Usually Dad gets deals on special cameras you can strap to your chest, but they're not really built for conversation. Not like a phone is.

'Listen —
if I did something to piss you off
before, on the climbing frame, I'm sorry.
The careers lady just gave me a SIM card
and a list of stuff I wasn't to do.
But she didn't really say what I should be doing, so.'

'Oh.' I can feel my palms getting sweaty. 'No, it's nothing you did. That sometimes happens with me. I . . . disappear.'

A disappearing girl.
Sounds familiar.
I can see the headteacher now

marching like a drill sergeant across the playground.
Her eyes
HUNT
for Mam,
but she won't find her.
Just me.
'What's your deal, then?
Why'd you disappear?'

I swallow and close my eyes and curse under my breath, because I know I have to be careful. If he learns about the Illness, he'll do his own disappearing act, just like my other friends did. Who wants to be chatting to someone who can't guarantee that she'll be able to turn up next time?

'I . . . I'm here to Live,' I say slowly. 'Through you. Whoever you are.'

He laughs in a way that sounds like rocks falling.

'I'm Rowan.'
Sorry to disappoint,
ghost girl,
but this ain't much of a life.

Suddenly the doors of the school open and hundreds of children in blue come splashing out on to the playground. Rowan stands up.

The headteacher's spotted me.
I can already tell

46

this meeting ain't gonna be good.
(What are you doing to me, Jonah?)
'Listen.
I've got to stream for you if I want to keep this phone.
If it's living you want, then fine.
Ten a.m. tomorrow, yeah?
Let's live.'

I watch as a smartly dressed woman beckons Rowan over from within a sea of blue sweaters, before the screen freezes and drops.

Rowan is no longer streaming.
Please choose another channel.

14

Alice

When I'm back to being entirely Alice again, I realize that Dad is already in the room, still wearing his work uniform and carrying a big box.

'Dad!' I snap my laptop closed. 'Haven't you heard of knocking?'

He lowers the box gently on to the chair and walks calmly out of the room without a backward glance, closing the door behind him. I feel guilty for a moment, wondering if I've finally managed to offend him, when I hear a knock.

'Oh, for God's sake,' I say as he pokes his head round the door, but he's already seen that I'm smiling. 'What do you want, anyway?'

He points to the box. 'It's Wednesday night.'

I look over to the whiteboard hanging up opposite my bed and under all the crossed-out words I read: PUPPY THERAPY.

My smile drops. 'You didn't . . .'

But Dad's busy, carefully opening the box and making noises no grown man should ever make as he lifts out a white Labrador puppy, who looks both bewildered and excited.

'But . . .' I say meekly as he brings it over, wriggling and trying to lick his face. 'My spoons . . .'

He stops, smile fading. 'Your mum said you were feeling better. I . . .'

And the way he's standing, holding the dog close to his chest, both of their faces drooping, I can't help it. Even though I can feel the conversation I just had with Rowan pulling at me, the remaining effects of the migraine, and all the hope I have for tomorrow at 10 a.m . . .

'Okay,' I say. 'Perhaps just a few minutes.'

Dad still looks unsure, but I hold out my hands for the dog and he passes it to me, tail wagging excitedly as it crawls all over my head and shoulders and licks my ears.

'Too much?' Dad says, and I turn to see that he's now holding a chocolate Labrador who's desperate to join the white one.

I can't help it. I give them each a spoon.

Puppy therapy = 2 spoons

And I don't know how many spoons I have left, but it's worth it to watch the dogs wrestle with each other, their tails whipping at my face. Dad sits on the bed with me and starts playing a game of what I think is hide-and-seek behind my legs, and I watch as the puppies leap over me and paw at him and his face lights up like it's Christmas.

'You did it without me!' Mum says, running in and jumping on the bed next to me, so both dogs abandon Dad and go tumbling over to her.

I laugh and put my hands out so I can feel them. Like soft toys fresh from the microwave. And I can smell dog food, and taste the fur on my tongue from where the chocolate one got his foot in my mouth, and I can safely say that it tastes nothing like chocolate at all.

But it tastes like Living.

And I can't wait to see Cecelia now. She might be able to climb walls, but her dad has never brought home puppies, or parrots, or even a python that one time . . .

'You didn't steal these, did you?' I say.

Dad gasps in mock horror. 'Me? A puppy stealer? My own daughter thinks I'm a common thief, Sophia.'

'Well, it has been known,' Mum says, sliding me a smile.

He puts his chin in the air. 'They're on loan from next door, actually. All above board, I'll have you know. Not like the python – that was a mistake, admittedly –'

Mum huffs. 'I'll say. I still get calls from that pet shop every time they lose an animal. They must have your mugshot up on the wall.'

Dad rolls his eyes. 'I *told* them I was borrowing it. I'm not a thief, you know.' He drops his voice as he picks up the white puppy. 'Although I might steal this dog. Do you think the Johnsons would notice if we paint Manta with that leftover emulsion from the kitchen and send him back in its stead?'

'Dad!'

Manta flicks his tail in anger.

Dad checks his watch and puts the dogs back in the box, before coming over to draw a line through 'Puppy Therapy' on the whiteboard.

We're all silent then, as he does that.

He stares at the board for a moment before writing something else under it, in such small writing that I can't read it from here.

It doesn't matter, though. The truth is, this board was once called the Cure Board. After a few years of trying different medicines and nothing changing, we started googling other ways we might banish the Illness. And the internet had a lot of ideas, actually. Thousands. Everything from eating strange herbs to living in a tent outside. We tried all of them and more – scoring them from the board when they didn't work.

And it got to the point when it was making everything worse, because here were loads of people saying that all I needed to do to be cured was do something like take a supplement, or change my diet, or do a special type of exercise. And when that didn't work, it was like them saying that I wasn't doing it right. I wasn't trying hard enough. That I didn't want to get better.

And it made me angry. It made us all angry.

So Dad decided to change the game into something less angry and more fun. Like borrowing the neighbours' puppies. Or whatever he's just made up and written down for next week. It's just a game now and won't make the slightest bit of difference to my health.

But there's still a quiet moment as we cross something off the list. Something that makes us realize that perhaps we were hoping just a tiny bit that we'd stumbled across a miraculous cure – however silly it might have seemed a few moments before.

Dad dims the lights and Mum hands me my earplugs before helping Dad with the box.

'You feeling okay?' she asks before she leaves.

And I don't need to lie this time. 'I'm feeling wonderful.'

15

Alice

I wake up early and spend an hour underwater.

It's my favourite documentary. I've seen this series a hundred times, but each watch reveals a new fish or flash of colour I've not noticed before.

That's the thing about the ocean. It's full of the best kind of surprises. And disappearing into this feels like sinking into a warm bath in which I can leave thoughts of speeding cars up on the surface, where they can't hurt me or anyone else.

When I first became Ill, I watched this series again and again on a loop. I was too unwell to even sit up in bed then, so I spent all my spoons on opening my eyes underwater. And I'd try to remember the names of the different fish and their behaviour – everything that would one day help me escape this room and dive into marine biology, where my greatest concern would be whale numbers and the mating habits of sardines.

However few spoons I have now, it's good to remember that I have so many more than I did back then. At least now I can move a little.

Morning physio = 4 spoons

Mum helps me stretch my arms and legs this way and that. And I have to push against her as I cycle an imaginary bike on the ceiling until my muscles collapse.

She picks up her handbag as I'm getting my breath back. 'Are you going to be okay today, sweetheart?'

She asks me this question every day, like I might have a breakdown between her leaving for work and coming home for lunch.

'I'll be fine – get lost already.'

She smiles and I kiss her powdery cheek as she bends over. 'Have a good day,' we say together.

And it's funny, because usually I watch her go and imagine the day she'll be having. Walking down our tree-lined street and hopscotching her way to the school staffroom to hold entire wild conversations about the terrible coffee and how awful teenagers are. But today I'm not wishing I was there.

I open my laptop. Today I have my own Living to do.

Connecting to **Rowan** . . .

16

Rowan

And now I am strapped to the chest of my new streamer, who's looking out on to the most perfect thing in the world, and I ruin the wonder of it all by screaming.

'Oh my days!'

'You swear like an old person.'

I tut at him, but it doesn't matter, because we're on *the beach*. And stretched ahead of us are miles and miles of the most beautiful sea – so calm that it could just be a puddle in the footprint of a giant. In the distance, a man on a stand-up paddleboard pushes himself lazily along towards the pier, which reflects flashes of morning sunlight like a disco ball into the water.

I can almost feel the stones under my own feet. I can smell the salt in the air and feel the spring sun, warm on my face. I want to take off my shoes and socks and paddle into the waves, walking to the part where the water turns from grey-blue to dark blue. I want to leave footprints on the seabed. I want to tangle myself up in the weeds. I want to swim over to the man on the paddleboard and ask him how his day is shaping up.

> *It's a bit of a shit way*
> *to start 'living'.*
> *A seagull is picking at a nappy*
> *someone's left in the bin.*
> *And all around are sirens and*
> *kids crying and*
> *my boss, Sue,*
> *hacking up a lung.*

He crosses his arms over a brown picket fence in front of him and leans into the wood.

'It's just how I remember it,' I whisper.

And somewhere there are dusty pictures of Dad and me taking out an inflatable dinghy on this very beach, trying to paddle our way round the pier. At some point, though, I'd miss swimming and Dad would get bored of rowing, and we'd both end up splashing into the water to run races and compete to see who could hold their breath the longest.

'Are we going to go in?' I say hopefully.

> *'Don't be crazy – I'll freeze my balls off.*
> *And anyway,*
> *I'm at work.'*

'Oh!' I say, and the picture of Rowan I had in my head jumbles into Wesley, making my chest pang. 'But I thought you went to school. How old are you?'

> *'Yeah, I do — I'm seventeen.*
> *I have a couple of free periods, though.'*
> *(And someone's got to pay the bills.)*
> *'I work the outdoor minigolf.*
> *See.'*

He turns round, and a whole world of treasure washes up on the beach. Green paths split with more brown picket fences, giant boulders, barrels and open chests. And, in the middle, an elephant with its trunk in the air, fountaining water into a pond.

> *'Usually I just work the desk all day,*
> *giving out clubs and stuff.*
> *But I thought we should have a game.*
> *You know,*
> *test the holes —*
> *make sure they still work.'*

I've not played minigolf in ages. The last time, I think, was with Cecelia when I was nine, and we only managed half the course because she kept climbing on all the obstacles and broke the nose off a dinosaur with her foot. I'm not sure I even remember how to play.

'Are you allowed to do that?'

I shrug.
'It's ten on a weekday
and it's bloody freezing.
Ain't like there's a queue.'

He holds up two balls to the camera, like fluorescent eggs.

'Orange
or yellow, um . . .?'
And I realize
I don't even know ghost girl's name.

'Alice,' I say, and I open and close my mouth a few times, hunting for the words that won't give me away. 'I can't play, you know.'

My heart is beating, beating.

'Well, yeah,
you're a camera.
But you can tell me what to do,
can't you?'

He says it and it sounds so simple, but it's not. All those years watching the other streamers Live for me, and I never once made a decision. I wasn't there to Live my life – just to come along for the ride while they Lived theirs.

And when they lost theirs, too . . .

Now I'm not only watching. I'm playing. I have a ball.

'Yellow,' I say, perhaps a little too loud. 'Please.'

I drop the orange ball first.
Hope she can't see the bit of fake turf
some kid chewed up with a club last week
that I was supposed to stick back down.
I steady my club.
Bend my knees.
SWING
and clip the side
so the ball just sort of wanders off.
I must have played this stupid hole
a million times,
but the camera's putting me off.

'You're not very good, are you?'

I can hear him sigh as he drops my yellow ball on to the plastic grass. It sits there like a sun waiting to rise.

'Go on, then –
you do better,
ghost girl.'

I'm frozen, because how can I? How can I hit a ball into a hole when I'm a girl stuck somewhere in a bed? A 'ghost girl'?

My thoughts panic and I remember a flash of a film Cecelia and I watched when we were too young, about a ghost who could walk into people and take over their bodies and feel their hearts beating inside their chest like they were Living again.

And perhaps this is the same, even though I'm far from dead. I can still cross over to the in-between.

'Grip the club lower down.'

I'm almost down by the floor at this point,
but okay.

'Pull it further back. More.'

You'd think she was out on an eighteen-holer
rather than a plastic jungle.

'Okay,' I say. And I can almost feel the club in my fingers – cold. Feel the sting in my knees from squatting. Feel the world vibrating under me like I'm standing on top of a speeding train.

'Go.'

I swing.
Or maybe she swings.
Anyway,
the ball blasts
left – right – left – right
RiCoChEtS
off a fake rock,
r o l l s
round the side of the hole
and
bottoms into it.

He's cheering and I'm cheering and the sea seems to roar along with us like an audience, with sunlight cameras flashing among the waves. And then an actual audience appears from round the front, waving money and gesturing at the gate stopping them from coming in.

Would you look at that?
Seems like ghost girl's brought this place
back to life.

17

Alice

It's movie night and I'm finding it difficult to concentrate.

Cecelia is sitting by the side of me, legs crossed over mine like we're flowers joined by the same roots. Dad keeps popping in uninvited to laugh at things I'm not entirely sure are jokes, and Cecelia is tutting away like she's a radiator that needs bleeding.

'Are we supposed to find this hero guy attractive? Maybe he was fifty years ago or something, but he's so old now it's like watching a boiled cabbage take down a drug ring. Seriously.'

I wrinkle my nose. The man is running around with a gun, shooting at people. And I think we're supposed to be laughing like Dad, but I can't help but wonder who the people are that he's stopping, and who they're leaving behind now they're dead.

It's making me think about Wesley. I've been trying hard to push him to the back of my mind into a dusty drawer, where I can focus on the brightly polished parts of the world. But now I have Rowan. And he's not just letting me watch – he's letting me be part of the game.

If Wesley had done that, could I have stopped it? Would I have told him to slow down . . . or speed up?

The not-so-attractive-any-more hero in the film lifts up a woman and kisses her, and Cecelia pretends to gag.

'Oh my God, love turns people into the grossest humans. This is like watching my parents get off.'

Dad pops his head in again, and Cecelia and I both shout, 'No!' before he can say anything inappropriate.

As soon as the kiss is over, we're back in a car chase again, whizzing our way through some American city, causing all kinds of carnage as people hang out of windows and shoot everything but the person they're trying to hit.

And as I'm watching the world in the film fly by, I see splashes of colour. Shops selling flowers. A person sitting on the pavement with a guitar and singing. A balloon that's uncurled from somebody's hand, floating up and up.

Wesley never saw any of that. He set his adventures by his watch. But if Rowan were the hero here, I think we'd be seeing everything differently. We'd have our noses in the flowers. We'd be listening to the music. We'd have our eyes on the sky.

Perhaps Wesley's note was right. There is something special about him.

'Well, that was crap,' Cecelia says as the credits roll. She turns off the TV and swings round to look at me, so our noses are nearly touching. She has this wild look in her eye – like she might take off at any moment – and I reach out and grab her arm, so I can float away with her.

'What did you do today?' she asks.

I think for a moment about the long recovery nap I took. The new meds I started. The time spent on my laptop. But she doesn't want to hear about that.

'I played minigolf. The one on the beach.'

Her eyes light up. 'The one with the elephant? You know, I bet I could climb that. Jump on the back of Jumbo.'

I nudge her. 'Break off its nose?'

'Hey,' she says, pointing at me. 'That dinosaur had it coming. That was an impossible hole.'

I laugh and push my forehead into hers.

'We should go and do something outside together sometime,' she says.

My heart drums up into my ears. 'Yes, maybe.'

She squeezes my face. 'And you know what's coming up, don't you?'

'My facial reconstruction surgery?' I say, wriggling out of her vice-like grip.

'No, stupid. My birthday! And it'll be my sixteenth, which will make me even sweeter. And I'm thinking I'll have a party. An actual party with beer and everything. BEER.'

My heart seems to stop and blast forward at the same time, and I miss a breath. I turn away, but she catches my wrist and squeezes it, tight.

'Come! It's just a small one, but it'll be so fun. Mum's leaving the house by some miracle, so we have free rein. Even of the hot tub, probably. As long as she doesn't find out. Come on, Alice, I know you don't like doing stuff with actual people, but live a little, yeah?'

Live a little. It gets harder to breathe.

She rolls over on the bed and whines and my throat is clotting with truths. Like how I spent my own birthday last month in this bed wearing a black funeral dress, watching my parents eat my birthday cake on my behalf, because I can't have gluten, or dairy, or sugar, or carbs, without crashing with a migraine.

Cecelia knows I'm Ill. She was there when I stopped going to school. She sees the empty pill boxes and the motor on my bed. But I keep having to remind myself that the reason she keeps asking me to do these things, like I have a choice, is because she doesn't know just how bad things are. She sees the good parts, where I'm sitting up in bed and able to hold a conversation. She hears my lies, telling her all the things I can only really dream of doing.

She doesn't know. And I can't tell her. I need her too much.

So I take a deep breath. Swallow the words down. Pretend that her hand gripping my wrist is Mum's.

I am safe. I am happy. I am alive.

I look at the crease forming above her nose. 'Sounds fun! Who else will be there?'

She takes a breath, before covering it with a smile and launching into a million-miles-a-minute monologue about all the people that have already said yes, who she'll need to keep apart and who might misuse the hot tub.

And I hope she noticed that I didn't actually say yes. That might make the inevitable last-minute excuse I'll give her a little more forgivable.

18

Alice

Welcome back to Stream Cast, Alice

Users online:

Rowan	**destroy_roy**	**tokyo--drifter**
Online for:	Online for:	Online for:
20 minutes	2 hours	7 hours

Users offline:

1mp0ssibledream	**WesleyCycles67**	**daddycool-007**
Last online:	Last online:	Last online:
1 day	35 days	85 days

Connect to a channel to start watching.

I sit, staring at the Stream Cast login screen for a while.

Usually I'd choose the streamer who's been online the longest. It only seemed fair to me, seeing as they'd taken the time to show me the world for so long.

The thumbnail by Hana's name is ripped with lines of colour, meaning that she's having signal issues again. And Living in short one-minute bursts and freezes is too distracting to really enjoy.

By the looks of it, Roy is still playing the same game with the guns and the apocalyptic landscape. I could try to get his number from my Auntie Holly – see if he'd mind playing something else for an hour a day . . .

But Rowan is online. His thumbnail shows a wide expanse of blue and – somewhere – a ball, waiting for me to hit.

I trace my mouse over the letters in his name.

'Sorry,' I whisper to Hana and Roy.

Connecting to **Rowan** . . .

19

Rowan

And now I am strapped to Rowan's chest as he sits on a beach, gazing out at a wide sky tumbling with bruised clouds. The sea looks angry, rolling grey and spitting froth. I can hear it roaring over the pebbles like a patient with a sore throat.

> *The weather is completely,*
> *royally*
> *shit.*

'Beautiful.'

> *She's online.*
> *'How are you getting "beautiful"*
> *from that?'*

'Well, look over there, at the horizon. There's a gap that looks like the sea's burning and all these clouds could perhaps just be smoke. And you can see it raining, even though it must be miles and miles away. It's like travelling in time or something, isn't it?'

I look.
And I want to see that.
All of that.
'All I see is rain coming this way,
to be honest.'

As he says it, thick drops fall from the sky, colliding with the beach like the whole world is caught in a dishwasher.

'Aren't you going to get inside?'

Sue's shut the golf,
so the only 'inside' is school.
And I've already bunked off for the day.
'You know –
you were better with the golf club yesterday.
Why don't you take a swing again?'

I can see the knees of his jeans getting darker and darker as the water hits him. And I want to tell him to stop being silly and get out of the rain before he catches his death.

But . . .

'Go on,
tell me what we should do. It's raining
and fucking freezing, to be honest.
Where we going?'

And –

It's as if I'm there with him on the beach as the rain gets harder and harder. It's like fingers thrumming to a rock band on my head. And I can feel the cold leaking into my bones and –

'Run!' I shout. 'To the pier!'

> *The water's in my eyes.*
> *I slide down the pebbles as I try to get up.*
> *I'm about as graceful as a newborn giraffe –*
> *but I'm running.*

And he – I – *we* – run. Ducking, like the rain might not reach us. Water slaps down our hair and slides under our feet. It dances on our tongues like loose change.

We're panting by the time we reach the umbrella of the pier and we shake ourselves like dogs.

> *I'm so unfit.*
> *'Can you still see?'*

Rowan smears the camera lens with the corner of his sweater.

'Did you get soaked?'

I imagine for a moment that he might turn the camera round – let me look at him drenched and dripping wet. And the thought of seeing his face makes my stomach flip.

> *I wring my hair out above the camera, so it*
> *h o s e p i p e s*
> *down.*
> *'That answer your question?'*

It almost feels like I, too, am soaked to the core, heart beating from running and rain dripping off my nose. And outside my own window, a mile away, I can see the same rain hammering, droplets blurring the bell tower in the distance to just a smudge.

We sit, curled up next to a huge metal foot holding up the body of the pier. Looking out, we can see rain curtains on either side, and other beachgoers screaming as they hold newspapers over their heads, darting into shops, their faces scrunched.

> *There's a hole in my shoe and*
> *the weather's leaking in.*
> *I'll just tape it up when I get back.*
> *Take another shift at the golf.*
> *I got this.*

Rowan gets up suddenly and shakes himself again.

'Are you cold?'

> *'Nah.*
> *It's my turn now.*
> *I want to show you something.'*

He turns round and we see a gate at the very back of the pier, barring the entrance to a dark tunnel under the road above, where killer cars tear through puddles and traffic lights flare.

He winds his fingers into the criss-cross bars and gives them a rattle. They don't budge.

I'm ready to walk away and perhaps try looking for something else to do while we wait for the rain to ease off, but Rowan traces his hand round the edge of the gate until he finds a latch.

'It's locked,' I say.

It always was.

He bends over, so all I can see is the zip of his hoodie, and I hear sounds like metal teeth chewing marbles.

'We're in.'
The gate
CREAKS
open
like a scary movie.

'Did you just break and enter?!'
And he actually laughs.

'Well,
we've not entered yet.'

He turns and I look around, checking for police officers and listening for sirens.

'You're as bad as my friend Cecelia. Locks are put on things for a reason, you know. It could be dangerous.'

'It's not dangerous.'

'How do you know? Like you said, you haven't entered yet.'

'Maybe not today . . .'

He takes the camera off his chest and I can hear his fingers tapping as if they're inside my head. Then suddenly a bright torch illuminates a whole tunnel of colour. Letters I can't read forming words that zigzag across the cracks. Eyes drawn on the ceiling that look down at us. Pennies, stuck with what I think might be chewing gum, reflecting the torchlight like the scales of a barracuda.

Rowan puts me back on his chest, but keeps the light on.

'So, what'll it be, Alice?
We breaking and entering?'

'I don't fully condone . . .'

I laugh, and it
b o o m e r a n g s
through the tunnel and back
as I swing the gate shut behind us.

We walk. More slowly than we would if we were above on the streets with the cars and the rain and the people. Even so, my heart is beating like it did after Cecelia broke the nose on that dinosaur and we ran away before anyone could see what she'd done.

This feels the same. We're hushed like we're hiding. Breathing like we're running.

We tilt our heads, reading the messages that different people have left on the walls.

'"Dance like no one is watching, 2013",' I read in red. 'My mum has that sign up in the living room.'

Well, at least I think she still does.

> *'Kimmi loves cock, 2011.'*
> *She tuts out of the speakers*
> *like an old lady.*

'Have you been here before?'

> *I swallow.*
> *'Yeah.*
> *I used to come here with my mam.'*
> *And I haven't been back, have I?*
> *Not since it happened.*

'Your mum?'

It feels strange that he would bring his mum to a place like this. If I ever picked a lock, I can't imagine my mum ever walking through. Dad, on the other hand . . .

The signal dips for a moment and I hold my breath. But when he comes back on, I see he's stopped walking and has stepped back, so the torch from his camera phone has washed out a wall ahead.

At the bottom, I can make out pots of paint and brushes, spray cans and rainbow stencils.

And then, as the light adjusts, I see it.

> *I don't know why I'm this nervous.*
> *She's just some girl*
> *at the other end of a camera.*
> *But I guess hers are the first eyes to see this*
> *since Mam's.*
> *And I wonder what she's going to see.*

It's a family of humpback whales.

The largest one is crashing through the waves at the top, fountaining a technicolour rainstorm from its blowhole. Its skin is crinkled with hundreds of different cracks and crosses, all wrinkled, up close, but then stretching wide into a giant from afar. And under its fins are two smaller whales, sheltered from the waterfall of yellows and oranges and reds above.

> *It's weird seeing it again*
> *after everything that happened.*
> *Like looking at a fairytale picture of how things*
> *should be.*
> *But instead here I am.*
> *Drenched to the core.*

'Did you paint this? And the kraken and the mermaid, too?'

> *'Once upon a time I did, yeah.'*

'They're beautiful. Really – they are.'

I kick a paintbrush.
'Thanks, but that's not really me any more.
I painted them for –'
I stop.
What am I doing?
Spilling my guts to some girl
I don't even know.
I clear my throat.
'What's your deal, anyway?
How come you're logging into my dumb life?'

My thoughts seem to tumble. And on my lips are lies and lies and lies.

'Oh, I'm helping my mum out,' I say quickly. 'She's the one who gave you this phone – she works at the school.'

So Alice is careers lady's daughter.
'Sent you to spy on me, did she?
You gonna tell her I'm bunking off today?'

'No! It's not like that. I'm just –'

I look round my room for inspiration. At the beige walls and Manta staring out from his little tank.

'I'm just at home. Home-schooled. This is . . . this is a project. For us both, I suppose.'

I scratch my neck.

'Yeah, well, there's probably better partners.
My life ain't exactly anything special.'

I look at the whales he brought to life on the wall.

'I don't know about that.'

Wesley was right. Anyone who could paint this must be special. And Rowan – he has no idea just how special he already is.

'You should keep painting.'

I look again at the whales.
At the smallest one at the bottom.
'It's not important,' I say.
'Not any more.'
These days
I've got bigger fish to fry.

20

Alice

I'm lost in fog.

After I said goodbye to Rowan, I spent hours thinking about the lie I told him, about this being a project.

The truth is that I used to be home-schooled. Mum and Dad even brought in a tutor for me, who would sit with me at the kitchen table as I struggled to pin numbers under my pen to stop them from wriggling off the page. But it got to the point where every session would take away spoons for days afterwards, until it felt like I was always breathlessly struggling to catch up.

I should be taking my exams this summer. But even just looking through the first page of the biology mock exam I keep on my bedside table is enough to make the brain fog descend.

Studying = 5 spoons

It hardly seems fair that I could drop spoons just by using my brain, but the Illness takes them all the same.

It's not a migraine, although they can hide in the fog. It's like standing in a forest but not being able to see any trees.

It's like stumbling on something and knowing what it is but forgetting the word for it. It's like being yourself and not being anyone at all, all at once. And all in a body that's battling with a sudden stuttering heartbeat, burning muscles and fever sweats.

I try to sleep, but I'm not tired. I'm exhausted. And I never realized how those two things could be different until the Illness hit.

I have something, though. A window. Before we left the tunnel, I asked Rowan to send me his phone number. And I have it now in my phone – a number that will stay in place no matter whether my brain can process it or not.

Through the fog, I send him a message.

Take me to school?

My phone buzzes like a ship's horn, blasting through the mist.

**Ugh. Okay. I need to show my face
there at least once a week, I guess.**

And that thought wraps round me like a life raft, keeping me bobbing on the surface until I can find my way back.

21

Alice

The fog has lifted, but it's left my limbs feeling dog-tired.

I try to sit up when Cecelia pops in, but I don't have the spoons.

She stops at the door. 'Oh man – migraine day again?'

I nod, because that's easier to explain. She comes over to lie with me in bed.

'You get these more than anyone I know. Maybe you should spend less time watching the wrinkly streamers? Too much screen time always brings my mum's on.'

I smile and bury my head in her shoulder. 'Shhhhh,' I say. 'Quiet time.'

She drops her voice to a whisper. 'Sorry. Let me show you what I've got planned for the party next Friday – that'll cheer you up.'

We lie silently as she flicks through images of rainbow cakes and playlists of songs we used to sing into hairbrushes. I rest my head next to hers and breathe in her body spray. Green tea. That was on the Cure Board once, but it didn't work. It still smells nice, though. Like home.

Cecelia and I used to have the best sleepovers. We'd stay up late, watching scary films and eating squirty cream straight from the can. We'd build forts in her bedroom out of pillows and sheets, all of them smelling like her. And although we had to take them down in the morning, those forts felt more like home than any other place I've ever been.

Even this room, with the cracks and imperfections I know like the back of my hand.

Cecelia's phone buzzes and I see a text from her mum flash up, shouting at her for not emptying the dishwasher.

'Bleugh – I gotta go before Mum flips her lid.' She kisses my forehead. 'See you on Friday, yeah?'

Wait. There was something I needed to say to her before her party. Something I needed to do. An excuse I needed to make.

I sort through the jumble of letters in my head for the right words. But her fingers slip through mine too fast to cling on to.

22

Alice

And now I am dreaming again.

I'm back under the water, feeling the pressure tight round my legs, my arms, my wrists. But I don't need to tell myself that I'm safe, or happy, or alive, because here, suspended in the middle of the ocean, I am.

But then I hear voices. Laughter. Coming from somewhere far away. And the sound is disorientating, like it's coming from all around me at once.

I spin and my chest bites. I feel myself starting to sink. And down below me the rocks are waiting.

I look up. Up to where my parents and Cecelia are talking. Laughing. Living. And I kick. Kick with all the spoons I have. But instead of going up, I sink faster and faster, until a rock suddenly juts up in front of me, slamming into my body like a tonne of metal, and –

23

Rowan

And now I am sitting at the back of a classroom splashed from all sides with crimson paint and chalk and splinters of clay.

I want to shout out. Ask Rowan about the walls hung with artwork, the swirls of ceramic flowers in the jars on the side, the pots stuffed to the brim with pencils and brushes. But at the top of his notebook he's writing letters in thick black pen.

> *SHHHH, I write.*
> *LEARNING.*
> *Although there's not much of that going on.*
> *At the beginning of the lesson*
> *the supply teacher just declared*
> *'free drawing'. Again.*
> *Honestly, if Alice hadn't asked me to come,*
> *I'd be leaving.*

I can see a tangle of wires hooking over the camera lens, and I think he's wearing headphones. I'm about to ask, when the person next to him moves.

'I'm bored,' says a girl with silver-tipped hair and a nose ring, lounging over Rowan's art book. 'What's with the new phone holder, dude? Is this some kind of protest about the no-phone-in-class rule? Because I'm with you.'

She stares into the camera and I feel myself blushing as if she can see into the lens, right through to me still dressed in my brain-fog pyjamas.

'Get off, Fran,' I say, shrugging her away.

The girl holds up her hands. 'All right, sorry, Mr Grouchy. But you know, if the supply teacher sees you with that, she's gonna confiscate it.'

She looks away, but keeps her elbow over Rowan's book.

'Is she your girlfriend?' I laugh nervously.

NO WAY, I scribble quickly,
shoving Fran off.
I draw a thick arrow to my right and turn
so she can see Fran's other hand
S Q U E E Z E D
in Charlie's.
And I don't know why it matters,
but I really don't want her to think –

'Oh,' I say.

Fran has turned her back on us now, lying in the lap of a tall boy with the same frosted tips – like they went halves on the same pack of hair dye. And then they kiss. In the middle of class. Hands wandering, eyes closed.

I wince. 'Do they do that a lot?'

> *I sigh.*
> ***ALL. THE. TIME.***
> *Since they got together last year,*
> *it's like my two best friends*
> *became one gross-out monster.*

The boy puts his foot up on the desk, kicking mud on to Rowan's book.

'Isn't there a teacher?' I ask.

> *I move Charlie's boot.*
> ***DEAD.***
> *The supply teacher couldn't care less*
> *about phones*
> *or anything else.*
> *She's marking at the front.*
> *Head down. Ignoring our existence.*

I grip the laptop in both hands.

> *I can hear a gasping sound through my earbuds,*
> *like a steam train gathering speed.*
> ***YOU OKAY?***

No. No, I'm not okay.

Because of course this was Wesley's classroom, wasn't it?
The red paint on the walls. Clots.

> *My mam used to make sounds like that.*
> *When things got really bad.*
> *I grab a paintbrush.*

I watch as Rowan flicks black ink from side to side on the page. Smudging greys and dotting specks of white into the corners. And, through the shadows, I see a frog balanced on a lily pad half submerged in the water. Its eyes peers out, glassy and unseeing, as its fingers clutch to stay afloat.

And it's good. Really good. But a whole world away from the kraken and mermaid and humpback whales.

'No colour?' I croak.

> *My paintbrush*
> *h o v e r s.*
> ***NOT ANY MORE.***

'How come?'

> *I could tell her.*
> *I could rip myself open and let her see inside . . .*
> *But I don't think she'd like what she'd see.*
> *The bell rings.*
> *Fran and Charlie unstick themselves from each other.*

'Wanna go hang?' the boy says, stuffing a clean notebook into a backpack. 'You can come round mine if you like – I've got that new Apocalypse game everyone's raving about. I'll let you play.'

I shake my head.
'Busy,' I say.

Fran throws her hands up in the air. 'But of course you are.'

I shrug. Wave.
And disappear into the crowd squeezing out of the door.

Rowan is no longer streaming.

24

Alice

I wake up with fewer spoons than I usually do. I can tell as soon as I open my eyes and it feels like my bones are made of lead.

I was haunted all night by images of Wesley trapped in a bleeding classroom and it's made focusing on all the wonderful things in my room this morning much more difficult than usual.

I just need a distraction. Something to turn the sunlight on my pillow golden instead of grey, and the sound of Dad crashing his way out of the door into an orchestra.

'Oh, chicken,' Mum says as she comes in and sees me. 'We'll get you washed and dressed and then you can spend the day resting.'

She starts the bed motor, but I reach over and stop it.

'I think I'll just have a pyjama day today.'

She frowns. 'It's not good for your mental health to be in your pyjamas all day – the doctor said.' She sets the bed going again, but again I turn it off.

She glares at me, so I muster a smile.

Pretending to smile = 1 spoon

She sits down next to me. 'What's going on, Alice? You've been so far away recently, it's like you're not really here.'

I want to tell her that's the point. That I'm Living outside of these four walls and there I can do anything. I can forget what it felt like to be with a man who died. I can keep being strong for both of us. But I can see the hunch in her shoulders from carrying so much of me already, so instead I lie.

'You know,' I say, smiling, 'you're right. Getting dressed is the best idea.'

She doesn't look sure, but I set the bed to go up again, and then say I need a few moments to stop feeling like I might faint. Eventually, we wait so long that her watch screams at her that she's going to be late for work.

'Perhaps I should call in,' she says, twisting her fingers together.

I swing a leg out from my covers. 'Don't be silly,' I say. 'I'm feeling better now I'm up. Get off to work and I'll get myself ready.'

She stands up. Then sits back down. 'You're sure that you're okay?'

I roll my eyes. 'I'm *fine*.'

She checks her watch again. 'I'm already late.'

'Go!' I shout, and this time she does, grabbing her handbag off the side and throwing me one more worried smile before she runs down the stairs.

As soon as I hear the front door go, I slip my leg back into bed and pick up my laptop.

Mum might need to look good on the outside to feel good on the inside, but I'm different. For me, feeling good means being outside. And today promises to have a great deal of that.

Welcome back to Stream Cast, Alice

Connecting to **Rowan** . . .

25

Rowan

And now I am watching Rowan scrape chewing gum from the side of an elephant.

I don't tell him I'm here right away. I just watch him chisel away at it with what I think is an old kitchen spatula covered in purple paint.

> *I swear*
> *I am never,*
> > *ever*
> > *buying a stick of gum again.*

'Do you use that spatula to paint?'
He jumps.

> *Ghost girl scares the bejesus out of me.*
> *I cough over my surprise.*
> 'Used to, yeah.
> *I used other stuff, too.*
> *Wooden spoons,*
> > *bottle tops,*

anything lying around, really.'

He stops scraping and I can see little flecks of dried paint on his skin now.

'Your house must be a swirl of colour.'

> *I dust my hands together.*
> *'A mess, you mean?'*

'No, I mean that it must feel like you're living in a painting, with everything being a brush.'

A sound starts to buzz like a swarm of angry wasps.

> *'Sorry, phone call.'*
> *The caller ID says INTERNATIONAL.*
> *Dad. Again.*
> *I decline the call.*

The buzzing stops. 'Who was that?'

> *I get out the sandpaper*
> *and start scratching at the gum stains.*
> *'You ask a lot of questions.*
> *What about you?*
> *Tell me something.'*

I clench my fists. 'What kind of thing?'

> *I shrug, pushing against the metal.*

'I dunno, anything.
Distract me.'

I look round my room and pick over my words carefully.

'I have a goldfish. His name is Manta. He's a Black Moor.'

'Okay . . . a fish.
That's something, I guess.
What else?'

Manta swims round in a panic.

'I . . . I like water. The sea. The ocean, actually. I watch a lot of documentaries.'

He puts his sandpaper and spatula in his bucket of loosened gum.

'The sea we can do.'

He stands and walks to the front of the minigolf course. The sky is the same colour as old tarmac, and see-saws as he steps.

'Hey, Sue –
all right if I take my break?
I've gotta be back at school at eleven, but . . .'

A woman hidden in the hut at the front is reading a newspaper. She holds a cigarette between her lips and looks at her watch.

'No point now, love. Might as well call it a day.'

Rowan puts the bucket on the desk and shifts from side to side. The woman looks up.

'Don't worry – I'm not going to dock you. Off you trot.'

> *Not gonna dock me?*
> *Usually she counts my pee breaks*
> *and now I get to leave an hour early.*
> *Paid.*

Rowan almost runs, away from the hut and the minigolf course, down the bank towards the sea – his shoes scattering pebbles and sinking up and down roller-coaster mounds as he heads to the water's edge.

The brown-grey waves stretch towards the sky.

> *The wind is wild.*
> *Kicking up a storm in my ears like rock music.*
> *'So there's the sea, Alice.*
> *What are we gonna do?'*

The sound of the waves is crashing into the microphone and I can hear a roaring – like the water has turned animal.

'I don't know . . .'

> *I spin round.*
> *I have an hour. An hour all to myself.*
> *And usually I'd just go and sit on the climbing frame.*
> *Wait it out.*
> *But with Alice the world seems different.*

New.
'Come on!
If you were here living,
ghost girl,
what would you do?'

I can feel my heart racing through spoons, because what would I do? What would I do if I hadn't got that silly virus when I was ten? If I hadn't felt the Illness tear me apart from my body and I had one that worked as well as the one I'm seeing now, with a whole world stretched out in front of it?

'I would be Living,' I splutter. 'With a capital L. I would be swallowing the world whole. I would dive to the bottom and climb to the top. I would squeeze the earth in my fists and plant myself down and let my roots clutch at everything, from the everyday to the extraordinary.'

The wind is trying to
WHIP
her weirdo words
AWAY,
but I hear them.
'With a capital L, eh?'
I look at the sea
chewing up the seabed
and I run back to the golf
to fetch something.

I'm feeling silly for saying all of that, because it probably wasn't very normal and he's started to run.

His boss raises her eyebrows as he charges up to her, but doesn't say anything as he unwinds a clear plastic bag with an orange string from the display at the back of the shop.

'I'll bring it back,'
I say as she shrugs.

He runs back towards the water, the world shaking from side to side. And I'm almost ready to apologize and tell him that he can do anything he likes with his time off, as long as I get to watch. But then I spot a shoe. And a pair of trousers. And I can't help but think about Cecelia's warning about men and cameras, so I shout, 'What are you doing?'

I must be going mad.
'Going in the sea.
That seems like an "Alice" thing to do, right?'

I choke on something because, yes. Yes. That's what I'd be doing. That's exactly what I'd be doing. And now I'm watching him doing it for me and I feel like I'm there, in my swimming costume, looking out at waves that want to swallow me whole and knowing that I'm strong enough to beat every single one.

'You can swim, can't you?'

I take off the camera strap
and my hoodie

and my T-shirt
until I'm standing on the beach,
shivering in my undies.
'I guess we'll find out.'

I shout out as the camera is shoved inside the plastic bag he took from the shop and sealed up tight, so I know that water can't reach it and my words can't be heard. But still I scream at him.

'Be careful!'

I watch his bright white hands as they wrap the string of the bag round and round his wrist, so no current can whisk it away without him going with it. So even if the worst does happen and he gets swept away to sea and loses his life – like the millions of people who've drowned in this very same water – at least I get to watch as his skin bloats and the bubbles stop coming out of his nose.

He's really shivering now as the wind whips up and the salt sprays.

Here we go.
I'm really doing this.
(Why am I doing this?)

And I'm afraid. It feels like my heart is beating a million times a minute.

It feels like Living.

I put my hand out. Imagine it wrapping round his. Imagine myself looking into his blurred, anyperson face and seeing eyes that see me. Really see me. And he'll see a person who knows how to swim. How to avoid the current and what to do if we get swept away.

A person who knows how to stay Alive.

And

together

we run.

Pebbles jab into the soles of our feet as we tumble down the bank of stones to where the weeds reach their fingers towards our toes.

And our feet splash into the very edges of the water and the cold bites and we cry out, but still we're running until the water swallows our calves and our legs and it gets harder to move and –

We dive. Into the wave that batters the beach, and we twist for air as the coldness takes breath from our lungs, and we want to shout out again, but our words have frozen. And all we can see is murky brown-grey and particles getting washed around as another wave crashes.

This time we get up. Stand on the seabed and breathe. And we think we have it all sorted when another wave comes and spins us back down again, into the brown nothing. And we can taste the salt in the back of our throats and feel it reaching to go further down. Down our windpipes. To make puddles in our lungs.

But together we're stronger than that. And we push ourselves up again, and this time, when the wave comes, we jump. And suddenly we're flying, higher than we could ever jump on land, soaring up to the grey clouds and the circling gulls and –

We're Alive.

And this time we take a deep breath and dive. Pushing past the brown murk to the seabed where seaweed sways like lost hair in a bathtub, and bubbles escape from under the sand.

And it's not like diving in the Caribbean. Or on the Great Barrier Reef. Or any of the places I dream about going swimming. But it's real. Real diving. Real swimming, as the current tries to tear us away from the beach and into its dark heart.

We stand up. Swallow another wave as it comes crashing in. And let it push us forward this time, so we're leaving the ice water and walking up on to the beach like the very first human, where the stones under our feet feel a lot more numb somehow and we can't stop shivering as the water drips from us.

And the camera string is unwrapped from our wrists and – I'm a watcher again.

Fuck,
fuck,
fuck,
it's cold.

I fall with the camera to the ground to look up at the clouds as a dark figure thrashes overhead, swearing and shaking while trying to wring water from his long hair. I squint at him, trying to make out his face, and feeling a jolt as I see the outline of a nose. A square chin. But it's too dark to see properly.

I can tell that he's shaking so much he can't get his socks on. But he shoves his feet in his shoes anyway, picks me up and marches off.

I.
Can't.
Even.

He walks. Up the beach and across a deserted road into a chip shop – sliding into a free booth in the corner.

Chip-fat steam
hits me like a train
and I can breathe again.

His shaking fingers lift me out of the bag and back into the holder round his chest.

The waitress comes over and we both say, 'Tea,' together, before she's even got out her pen.

'Rowan? Are you okay?'

That was
WAY
colder
than I thought it'd be.
'I might go to the bathroom.
Run my hands under the hot tap.'

'Don't be silly, you'll lose your fingers.'

> *I whimper like a dog*
> *before I can stop myself.*
> *'How do I get warm, then?'*

'Dry yourself off more. Try to put your socks on. The tea will help.'

He does that while the waitress brings the tea over in a styrofoam cup and Rowan wraps his blue fingers round it.

'Better?' I say.

He lets out a shuddering breath.

> *'So that might not have been the best idea, huh?'*

I try not to laugh, because he's cold and wet while I'm still warm in my bed and feeling wonderful.

'It was very sweet of you, though, to do that for me.'

> *This tea tastes like plastic,*
> *but feels like lava in my chest.*
> *'It was for you, but I think*
> *I did it for me, too . . .'*
> *And I can't remember the last time I said that.*

It's getting more and more confusing to know who's who. And I hope that feels as wonderful to him as it does to me. Like the lines between us are blurring and I might reach out, through the camera, and wrap his blue hands in mine.

'There are so many more things we could do,' I say.

He blows over the top of his tea.

'We could go paragliding. Or to a rock concert. We could hop on a ferry, or a train or maybe even a plane. We could go to Australia to learn to dive and swim with manta rays.'

I'm getting excited now, because all the things I'd forgotten that I wanted to do – because they were laced with the thought of not being able to do them and shut up in a drawer at the back of my mind – are flooding back to me.

She says it like
anything really is possible.
That's what made me jump in the water.
I wanted to feel that.
Now I'm just back to feeling cold.
'Yeah, maybe we'll rob a bank first, eh?
Steal a few mill.'

'Well . . . maybe not Australia, then. But there's a whole world of things we can do here, I'm sure.'

I put down my tea, because I'd forgotten.
This girl –
Alice –
she's not
AFRAID
of what will happen if she
– loses her job or
– can't pay the heating bill or

– someone finds out and takes everything away.
Alice has a mam to do all that stuff for her.
'That ain't real Living, you know.'

I lose track of my thoughts and they circle.
'What do you mean?'

'You can't just
DO
all that.
There's consequences.'

I think of migraines and fevers lurking at the end of a busy day. And I watch him pour enough sugar into his tea to perhaps kill me off altogether.
'I know all about consequences.'

I'm cold.
I'm wet.
And I want to show her she's wrong.
'Fine.
Come back online 3.30 tomorrow.
I'll show you real Living.'

Rowan is no longer streaming.

26

Alice

It's the evening. Dad is downstairs doing the washing-up, which you can tell because it sounds like he's conducting a brass band with out-of-tune whistle solos.

I'm trying to wrap Cecelia's birthday present, but my arms aren't moving the way I want them to and the tape keeps sticking to itself.

I think she'll like what I've made for her, though. It's taken spoons and spoons over weeks and weeks, but it's finally finished.

It's a scrapbook. Filled with photos of us from the first day we met at a school sports day, when we came joint first in the long-jump competition and refused to share the medal. All the way to this Christmas, when Cecelia joined us for our traditional Boxing Day fry-up. And I've stuck other things in there, too, like the ticket stub from the minigolf when she broke the dinosaur, and shells we picked up from the seabed that time we went to Wales together.

It's a whole life stuffed into a book. And it's nearly killed me to make it, but I need it to be amazing if she's ever going to forgive me for this . . .

So sorry, I've caught a cold –

I delete it. She'll never let me off for just a cold, even if that is usually enough to take spoons for weeks and weeks.

I can't come Friday night ☹ – family
emergency.

I'm just wondering whether I can convince Dad to lie for me when he appears in my room, a tea towel flung over his shoulder.

'Dad, what do you think about –'

He marches to the bed, sticking his face right in mine. 'Spoon count.'

There's this look in his eye. It's a look I remember from when we were at the top of mountains on bikes and he would search me, making sure I had the gall to go down the slopes without falling off.

'Five,' I lie.

Silently, he reaches under me, lifts me up. I drop my phone before I can send the text.

'Hurry!' Mum whispers up the stairs.

He carries me out of the room and I try to read what he's written on the Cure Board for this week, but it's too small. But whatever it is, it makes him take me out on to the landing. And down the stairs.

I hold my breath and grip him, tight.

Holding on to Dad = 1 spoon

I can feel Dad's body working like a piston to carry me, and I can smell all the cooking smells from dinner mingled with lemon washing-up liquid. I try to take it all in as we go, because it seems like ages since I was down here, but things have been frozen all this time. The phone balanced on a stack of magazines on the hall table. The living-room sofa with the rip in the seat that Dad keeps saying he's going to fix but never quite gets round to. And the patio doors, thrown open like we're in the middle of a summer's day.

Being downstairs = 2 spoons

My heart is beating fast now, because I can see that it's dusk outside, and the world is ocean-blue. Dad readjusts his hold on me and carries me through the living room to the doors.

'Outside?' I gasp, clutching hold of his neck, tight.

Mum's there, waiting with a sunlounger.

'It's a bit late for sunbathing.' I laugh shakily as he lays me down on it.

They both kneel next to me as I take in the shadows in the garden – the shed at the bottom, emerging from the back like a huge ship. The flower borders. The washing line. My swing, rusting and covered in spiderwebs. It's all still here, waiting for me.

And my whole body is quivering because I'm *outside*. Me in my own body. And it's dealing with it just fine, albeit a bit unsteadily, but that's pure excitement, I think.

'Look,' Mum whispers, tilting her head back.

I wrench my eyes away from my old swing and up into the sky, where the very last of the light is leaking through the clouds. Suddenly something flutter-darts over us. As I move my head to follow it, another darts out, swinging from behind the house and flapping above our heads in a way that whispers.

At first I think it's a bird. But as one swoops down so close that I could reach out and grab it, I realize that it's a bat. A black streak in an ink-blue sky. And, as I keep looking, I see more. Three, four, five. All swooping over the garden like they're paper in water.

I squeeze Mum's hand, but we don't say anything because we're underwater, too. The world is silent now and it's just us, in a garden, looking up at the world as it Lives.

And I feel that Living breathing on my toes. I feel it hard under my back. I smell it as something cold and freshly cut.

For one moment, I have been pieced back together. Me and my body. And I am Alice and I am Alive.

When the final light leaks out of the sky and I stop being able to feel my toes altogether, Dad scoops me up again.

'Just a moment longer,' I say.

'Another time, kiddo.'

I watch through the window as we walk away. But he doesn't take me to bed right away. Instead, he lays me on the sofa, head in his lap and legs over Mum's, and we watch TV with the subtitles on. It's just some game show, and Dad shouts the answers out and more often than not he's wrong. And Mum boils some eggs and we peel the shells off them together, dipping the eggs in salt and mayonnaise.

I look around and see Mum still has that sign up. *Dance like no one is watching*. And on the window sill are whole lives laid out and popped into photo frames. Of them dancing together at their wedding. Of them standing on top of the Great Wall of China and smiling like they, too, could be seen from space. Mum onstage with the Splice Girls, and Dad getting his red belt in tae kwon do.

And then there's me, severing them down the middle. And the photos turn from baby pictures – trips to the local farm – to swimming galas. And finally me on my sixteenth birthday, lying in bed, holding the glass of champagne that gave me a migraine.

They gave up everything for me. My parents. They could be doing wonderful things, and instead they do them all for me. And it makes me feel awful and amazing and loved and devastated all at once.

But being down here with them feels more like a cure than any of the tablets, or supplements, or weird slimy things I've ever taken. Perhaps not for the Illness, because that's there somewhere, taking spoons, as it always does. But there are perhaps different kinds of cures. Cures for worries.

And, for a moment, I'm lifted out of fatigue and pain and tumbling spoons. And it's like my life is carrying on along the window sill.

27

Alice

I wake up feeling like I never went to sleep.

Mum can tell, despite my smiles. She leaves the curtains closed and cuts my salmon into small pieces so I don't need to drop more spoons than I have. And she doesn't ask me how many that is, because on days like this it's difficult to know.

'No laptop for you today, I think,' she says, and she wraps the lead round it like a chain, before putting it on the desk on the other side of the room.

It might as well be in Tokyo, all the way over there.

I know she's right, though. I know the only thing waiting on the other side of pushing through a day like this is even fewer spoons for the next. And the next.

But yesterday I got to go outside. Not as anyone else. As me. As Alice.

And even though I'm paying the price for that now, I want more. The fog is rolling in and creeping past my toes and my knees and my thighs. But I have Rowan at 3.30 p.m. today. He's promised that he'll show me what real Living is like and I'm going to do whatever I can to reach him.

So I don't move all day. I doze, dreaming of cycling down mountains on the back of the wind, and startling from sleep when a car comes from nowhere and shatters me again. And I put my hands on my wrists and try to focus on being happy, and everything being perfectly brilliant, so I can keep thoughts of Wesley away.

And then, at 3 p.m., I put one foot out of bed.

At 3.10, I set the bed to upright.

At 3.15, I blink away the spots and swallow the pressure pinching at my shoulders, and I drop, as carefully as I can, on to the carpet.

And then I crawl. Slowly. Trying to keep my breathing even. One hand out.

Move.

One hand out.

Move.

And I make it all the way to the desk with five minutes to go, so I reach up and try to steady my hand. I grab the laptop by the lead and pull it down.

Getting the laptop from the table = an impossible number of spoons

I made it all the way over here. And I'm both relived that I could and angry with myself for even trying, because I know it won't go unpunished.

I open the laptop and lay my cheek on the carpet so the thumbnail by Rowan's name is tipped on its side.

Connecting to **Rowan** . . .

28

Rowan

And now I am in that place we were before. The playground.

> Jonah's rocketing around like
> nothing matters.
> I watch him from the window of the
> castle climbing frame.
> And in the distance I see the line of grey sea
> Alice once saw for me.
> Like she sees most things I can't.
> I check the app again and –
> 'You're online?'

Yes – I want to say. Yes, I'm online and I'm here.
But my voice isn't quite . . .

> 'Alice?'
> She's definitely online.
> Her name is traffic-lit go.
> I turn the volume up.
> 'I think there's something screwed with your sound.'

But there's nothing wrong with his.
Birds.
Laughter.
Creaking swings.

Nothing.
Maybe she's having connection issues.
I was regretting saying that she could be here, anyway.
I wanted to show her what it's really like
— to live in the real world
— to have someone depend on you
— to be there for them. No matter what.
But even though she seems cool,
her mam could just make
o n e c a l l
and my brother,
he'd be —

Rowan swings his legs between the mermaid tail and slides down to the birthday cake floor.
We are weightless. We are free. We are flying.

Jonah!
Time to go.'

A yellow-headed boy kicks himself off the swing, runs to Rowan and pulls on his arm.
'Oh, but please,' he says. 'You said five more minutes.'

'Yeah, that was fifteen minutes ago, wasn't it?'
He cries and
sinks to the floor and
this is what his headteacher was talking about.
'Come on, mate, don't do this now.'
He's wailing louder and
other mams are looking over,
shaking their heads.
I got this. I got this. I got this.

There's a boy on our arm. A boy stopping us from flying.

'How about we hit Tesco on the way back,
get an ice cream?'
He stops crying so I take my chance and
LIFT HIM
high into the air and on to my shoulders
and he shrieks, laughing.
He's getting too heavy to carry like this.

Small shoes kick my camera.
  'Can we go up there?'
  'Up there' is out of my view.

He points up to the bell tower again.
Always. Always with that tower.
'Not now, mate.'

I am watching I am watching I am watching.

I'm supposed to be in between. I'm supposed to be both.
The boy wails for me. 'But when, then?'

> *Never again.*
> *Never again.*
> *Never, ever again.*

I watch as my window goes into Tesco. Grabs a trolley.

> *I let Jonah down, feeling breathless*
> *like I did when I was running in the rain with Alice.*
> *I check my phone for her name again.*

I remember supermarkets. So many things on the shelves.

I want to tell Rowan to get whatever he wants. Chocolate.
Custard. An entire garlic baguette.

But instead –

> *I stuff my Alice-free phone in my pocket.*
> *'Go on, then, Jonah.*
> *Choose whatever you want.'*

You have disconnected from this stream.

29

Alice

Mum found me lying in the middle of the floor and I don't think I've ever seen her that furious before.

She was shouting at me. Not her usual soft scolds, but yells that took spoons from my ears when I didn't really have any left to give. Dad had to send her out before he could lift me back into bed.

'What are you doing, giving your mum a fright like that?' he said.

I just looked at him at the time, because I didn't really understand what he was saying. The fog had moved up over my chest and was wrapping round my thoughts by then, smothering them.

But now it's the next day. Almost evening. And I've clawed back enough spoons to say, 'I'm sorry.'

Mum doesn't look at me. Just carries on folding my clothes neatly. Stacking them in the wardrobe. 'I didn't mean to shout. It was just a shock seeing you there. I thought –' She stops what she's doing.

'I'm sorry,' I say again. And I am. Usually I hide the worst of things from her well enough, but there was no hiding yesterday.

She looks tired as she comes to sit on the side of my bed, giving me a watery smile that dribbles down her face.

'What were you doing? What was so important?'

She looks like one of those rabbits that magicians pull out of hats. As if she can't quite work out how she got here, and isn't quite sure what to do now she is.

'I can't remember,' I say, avoiding her eyes so she doesn't see Rowan's name in mine and take him away again.

She sighs. 'Well, that's it now, okay? If you don't have the spoons to get up, then don't try. At least unless one of us is here with you.'

I nod and kiss her cheek as she leans down to do the same to me.

And I wait until she's out of my room and all the way back in hers before I dig my phone out from under my pillow.

Ten per cent battery remaining. I feel like I have the same. It should be enough to speak this time at least.

I download the Stream Cast app. Log in.

Welcome back to Stream Cast, Alice

Users online:

destroy_roy

Online for:
3 hours

Rowan

Online for:
5 hours

Users offline:

tokyo--drifter

Last online:
18 hours

1mp0ssibledream

Last online:
1 day

WesleyCycles67

Last online:
39 days

daddycool-007

Last online: 89 days

Connect to a channel to start watching.

Connecting to **Rowan** . . .

30

Rowan

And now I am watching as Rowan rolls socks with dinosaurs on them and puts them away in a rickety old drawer.

I clear my throat.

> *I scream.*
> *Then try to pretend that I didn't.*
> *'Al-Alice.'*
> *I take a breath.*
> *'You're back?*
> *You're okay?'*

'I'm back. I'm okay.' I laugh nervously. 'Hello.'

> *'Hi.'*
> *I'm pleased she can't see the*
> *thousand times*
> *I've checked my phone in the last day.*

'Thanks for taking me back to the mermaid again yesterday. I'm sorry my . . . my sound wasn't working.'

She was there, then.
And now my cardiac is over
I realize that she's here, too.
In Jonah's bedroom.
Watching me fold his washing.

He drops a pair of socks and I lean down to pick them up, before remembering that I'm a whole world away.

'Um – hold on.'
I bend.
Pretend that my hoodie is accidentally
covering the camera lens,
but keep my finger pressed over it.
I run into the hall –
close the door on Jonah, who's watching TV in
Mam's unused bed –
and into the living room.
Then I stand in the centre and spin.
Torn armchairs.
Cigarette-melted wallpaper.
Lego all over the carpet.
I turn to face the window.

I'm back up for air after swimming in a grey sea, and now I can see a dark window over a sideboard with a black-and-white chequered top, photo frames balanced on the squares like they're in the middle of a game.

'So the mermaid – yeah.
It's one of my favourite places, that.
My mam used to take me there after school –'

'Are we in your house?'

I'm looking for purple paint flecks, but I can't see any. The wallpaper is an ink spill of yellows and golds, but not quite how I imagined it would be. I thought Rowan's life would be like living in a painting come to life. But this? This could be my room.

Shit shit shit.
'Yeah, listen –
you probably saw that I have to –
um –
BABYSIT
a lot.
My little brother, Jonah.
I'm kind of in the middle of that now, so . . .'

I try to see round him, out of the window. Outside there are street lights like yellow stars.

'Where's your mum, then?'

I swallow.
'She's, um –'
It would be so easy to lie to her
like I lie to everyone else.
'She's not here.'

I close my eyes.
(What am I doing?)
'She's never here, actually.
She left. About a year ago.'

A car goes by the window and the lights flicker over the photo frames.

And I see a baby being held between a man with a beard and a woman with rosy cheeks.

A toddler, with thick dark hair, finger-painted every colour under the sun.

A kid's drawing of a boy and his mum – holding hands and jumping into a swirling universe.

Gone – left.

'Oh . . .' I whisper, my heart sinking. 'And your dad? He –'

I think of all those missed calls.
'He walked out ages ago.'

Rowan shifts his arm and I see the rest of the photos on the window sill. And – just like with the pictures in my parents' living room – the photos of Rowan's life are cut short by another: a boy with bright yellow hair.

It feels like my lungs are leaking air.

'You look after him, don't you?'

My breath catches.
Just one word.
Just one.

And yet it could
b r e a k
everything.
(I shouldn't tell her. I shouldn't.)
'Yes.'

I see it now, I see it. His brother. His brother is stopping him from Living.

Just like I'm stopping my parents.

I press myself against the wall, waiting for
— the knock on the door
— the sympathetic looks
— the 'we'll take it from here'.
I got this, though. I got this.

My breathing's going funny.

'You could be a great artist, you know,' I blurt.

Huh?
'What does that
have to do with anything?'

I'm losing my grip on my thoughts. My chest feels . . . wrong.

'I just mean — you could be something special. You could —'

'Alice — what . . . ?'
I told her.
I ripped myself open.

Showed her the broken pieces inside.
And I don't think she's looking.

My thoughts fog.
　'Don't let looking after him stop you.'

Something inside me –
something old –
snaps.
I take the phone out of the holder.
'No.
You don't get to say that, Alice.
You don't know –'

'I know,' I say.
　I feel it like a thousand tonnes of water pressing on my
bones.
　And it feels like sinking.

There's a
C R A S H
from Mam's bedroom
and Jonah starts crying.
'I don't need this.
Go and find your own life, Alice.'

Rowan is no longer streaming.

31

Alice

I come off the stream and something's wrong. Something's wrong.

My heart is fluttering. Fluttering. I'm gulping air. At least I think I am. I'm watching Manta in his tank and he's doing the same, but he is gulping water. Water, into his body and out through his gills. Only I don't have those and maybe that's why I feel like I'm drowning.

My hands are earthquaking, but I put them over my face to make sure my mouth is open, and it is.

And then the door opens. And for a second it's like breaking the surface of an impossible sea, because I'm sure that it's Mum or Dad and they always know how to bring me back up to the surface.

But it's not them. It's Cecelia. She's a blur of anger and mascara lines. A twisted glitter dress and a bright blue can.

'Ce–'

She slams the door closed and the sound is a knife in my ears.

'You didn't come,' she slurs quietly. She's swaying in the middle of my room, too far away to cling on to.

I open my mouth wider and try to ask her to get help. *Get help. Please.*

She's wearing a plastic crown made of little pink stars and she wrenches it off her head and throws it at the wall so the stars rain like an exploding sky over my body trapped under the covers.

She doesn't understand. She doesn't –

'You're supposed to be my best friend!'

Her voice is louder now and it's *knives knives knives.*

I close my eyes and hear thunder feet stomping towards me as hands grip my wrists.

I am safe. I am hap–

'You said you'd be there. You said it, you said – Look at me!'

I can't, because the light is on and it's spitting sparks into my eyes. But also she can't see. She mustn't see. I can't let her see this.

I try to speak. Try to explain that I'm not sure what she's talking about and if she could just explain . . .

'My sixteenth birthday. That's supposed to be special, you know. Sweet sixteen.'

Her sound has emptied so the words are forming now into things that I understand. And my insides plummet.

Her birthday party. It was today.

I open my eyes.

She has glitter eyeshadow tracks down her face to her chin. Her eyes are pink.

The text. I never sent her the text.

'Go on, then. What's your excuse this time? You were too busy, right? Or – or maybe you were off dancing with the leprechauns, or away with the lie fairies, or –' She throws her arms around so the can she's holding tips liquid on to the carpet and I smell beer.

I want to say. I want to say that my excuse is that I'm bedbound by an Illness that is trying to take everything from me. School. Friends. A future outside these four walls. And I want to say that I'm fighting it with all the blunt things I have and that I really, really did want to go. I really did. But that she might as well have held that party on the moon for all I'm able to get there.

But I can't say that. Not only because then the Illness will take her, too – and she's the one I'm so desperately trying to keep. But also because the Illness has taken my voice again.

I gurgle at her and her face twists.

'You know, I really thought you'd make the effort for this one.'

And that look in her battering-ram eyes . . .

I crumble.

The door opens and it's Mum, but it's too late.

'Cecelia, I said no visiting.'

Springs uncoiling in the bed.

A sniff. 'I was leaving anyway.'

Stay, stay, please stay.

Footsteps out of the room
    down the stairs
        into shoes
           and out of the door.

'It's okay, sweetheart, she's gone,' Mum says, turning off the light, putting earplugs in my ears and checking the alert on my heart monitor that is beeping, beeping.

But it's not okay.

Cecelia's not okay and neither is Rowan.

And I . . . I am –

32

Alice

Light

shining.

Knives.

Look.

Through the fog.

Mum.

Dad.

A woman

speaking.

What are words?

I should say hello.

Hello.

I am Alice.

I appear to be

lost.

Can you help?

But then

I see

a stethoscope.

A doctor.

No.

No, she can't help.

They never can.

But no matter.

I know my way around here.

I come here often.

The trick

I always find

is to choose something to

cling to.

Think.

Where's your skin?

What's burning?

Pins-and-needles legs.

Sore throat.

Hot hot hot.

But hands.

Something in my hands.

It's Mum.

Mum's hands.

I can tell

by the wedding ring.

I hold them.

There.

I'm not lost.

Let the doctor measure

and check

and ask her questions.

Let her prescribe

plenty of fluids and rest.

And leave.

Then Mum

and Dad

can find me.

Bring me back

to the land of the Living.

33

Alice

Mum has red eyes and I know that means someone has called her a bad parent again.

I put out my hand and find hers and it's cold. I give it a squeeze.

'How long?' My voice sounds like it might disappear again.

She strokes my fringe out of my eyes. 'It's Tuesday morning. I've called in sick, but your dad had to go in. He's going to take tomorrow off, though.'

I want to shake my head and tell her that I'm fine, but I think that's too big a lie today.

I feel awful. Hot and cold and shivery. Dizzy and sick and wobbly and like everything is happening to me all at once.

'What happened?' I squint and Mum lets go of my hand for a moment to put my sunglasses on. Even though the curtains are closed and my earplugs are in and I'm out of the scratchy sheets and into the silk ones, it still feels like I'm on a merry-go-round at full speed.

'One spoon-drop too many, we think. But then your blood pressure got dangerously low and that's a new one, so we called the emergency doctor out.'

I look at her, dark now through the glasses. And I don't need to ask her why she's been crying, because I know what would've happened. It's happened before.

The doctor would've wanted to take me to hospital. And hospitals were a good place to be when I was seven and I fell out of a tree, breaking my collarbone. Back then, they did an X-ray, showed me the lightning bolt in my milk-white bones and sent me away in a sling until it mended. And although it felt like the worst pain at the time, I would take a thousand collarbone breaks if all they had to do to fix the Illness was take an X-ray, see the crack and promise it'll be healed in six to eight weeks.

But that's not what hospitals do now, because the Illness is a shadowy beast. It hides in X-rays and shows up as a slightly unusual shape in an MRI. So your parents spend a lot of money they don't really have getting doctors to keep looking, looking, until they tell you that you don't have the thing you thought perhaps you did. Then they'll do blood tests and colonoscopies and endoscopies and biopsies, and, whenever anything comes up 'abnormal', you're happy – because you think you've finally found its hiding place. But then it'll turn out just to be the Illness's tail. Or the footprints it leaves behind.

But the doctors keep you in, anyway, to monitor you. And when you don't get any better, they start asking different questions. Questions about what could be going on in your head to mean that you're not well. Questions to Mum and Dad about why they're allowing their daughter to sit in bed all day. And those are the questions that take spoons from parents, too.

I squeeze Mum's hand tighter.

I didn't get taken to hospital this time at least. Mum and Dad must have said something and the doctor must have listened.

But I also feel awful, because this one was my fault. I pushed too hard. I ignored my spoon count. I wanted to Live so badly that I forgot that real Living isn't the same now as it used to be. As it is for Rowan and Cecelia.

And I hurt them, too. Both of them. And I feel that like fire running through the hollows of my bones.

'It's not your fault, sweetheart,' Mum says.

She pinches my wrists lightly between her fingers and thumbs. But it doesn't work this time.

34

Alice

She comes in like a whirlwind and I can't find a breeze to help me move.

Cecelia. Her usual bright colours have been washed out to a navy blue hoodie and stonewash jeans. And I'm here in this bed, wired up to machines that beep – my hair having only had a dry-shampoo wash in days and I generally still feel a little bit like death.

She had her chin in the air and a thunderstorm face when she first slammed open the bedroom door, but now she's frozen – her fingers still on the handle.

And she sees.

I try to sit up. Try to hide the Illness from her. Try to smile and make room for her to fill my space with hers, just for a little while. And I try to say that I'm sorry.

But I can't do any of it. All my spoons are fighting the Illness today. So all I can do is lie there, and look, and fall impossibly far without moving an inch.

Dad comes up the stairs behind her. 'How'd you sneak in?' He offers her a sausage from his plate, but she's still staring at me like she's discovered a dead body.

Dad shuffles past her into my room, humming to himself, and I try to catch his eye and tell him, *Don't let her see. Don't let her see this.*

'Come to make this one feel better, have you? That's good of you.'

He sits on the bed and takes the plate of sausages and starts cutting them up small and it must be lunchtime and oh no.

No, no, no.

Cecelia's eyes are wide and she's gripping the door frame like she, too, might fall over. And she watches as Dad opens my jaw for me and places a tiny amount of food in my mouth.

And I think about what she must be seeing. Her friend, who always just seemed a bit tired and overdramatic, being fed like a toddler. Hooked up to machines her parents bought on eBay so they could turn her bedroom into a hospital. Looking like it might be too much energy to keep her eyes open.

Cecelia clears her throat. 'What happened to her?'

Dad smiles and pats the side of my bed, but she doesn't come closer. 'Ah, just the old spoon wobble. We've not had one in – what is it, Al – two months? New record, I think.' He bends down close to me, still smiling. 'We're going the right way, eh?'

Please stop talking, Dad. Please.

Cecelia lifts her chin. 'Spoon wobble?'

'Yeah, you know,' Dad says, not understanding my eyes. 'She did a bit too much, that's all. My fault really – I took her downstairs. Sophia told me it was too much, but it's bat season. Have you got any round yours?'

'Downstairs is too much?' she says, her voice croaking now.

And Dad swings round to look at her like she's made a joke. 'Where have you been?'

She's been here. Here, with me. Bringing the outside world in for one beautiful moment and leaving before she got to see what life on the inside is really like. Hearing my lies about tae kwon do and gaming and exploring cities – all the things I told her I did, but only ever really watched.

She looks afraid.

Tell her it's not contagious, Dad.

Tell her that I'm still the same Me, trapped in here.

Tell her that I'm sorry.

Dad feeds me another mouthful. But it's a bit too much and I choke.

By the time I've stopped coughing and look back to the door – she's gone.

35

Alice

I'm back.

Perhaps not entirely, but enough to climb into the bath and wash the Illness from my skin. Enough to feed myself. Enough to feel the gap that Cecelia has left since she's been gone.

> I'm sorry I didn't make it to your party!
> Had the worst flu – bet I looked like
> death when you saw me.

I spend a long time trying to get the perfect balance of light and breezy and lies. But I can't have done a very good job, because she doesn't reply.

> Why don't you pop round after school
> later? I have your birthday present!

Nothing. Nothing.

I don't text her again, because this is how it went before, with the others. They came round with their parents and visited me. And we had so much fun, playing games on my computer and watching videos on their phones. But then they'd invite me somewhere and I'd say no. And no. And no. And soon they stopped inviting me. Then they stopped visiting altogether.

But Cecelia never did that. She kept coming and letting me steal moments with her and it was everything. And I thought that if I hid the Illness from her, and lied about what I could do, then she wouldn't leave like the others did.

If only I'd sent her that text – I was never going to be able to go to her party. I know that and it's okay. Really it is. Because that's the way things are, and there are plenty of wonders to be seen from a bed.

Welcome back to Stream Cast, Alice

Users online:

1mp0ssibledream	tokyo--drifter	destroy_roy
Online:	Online:	Online:
40 minutes	3 hour	5 hours

Users offline:

Rowan	WesleyCycles67	daddycool-007
Last online:	Last online:	Last online:
10 days	49 days	99 days

Connect to a channel to start watching.

I hover over the people online. I could do hook kicks in a tae kwon do tournament, spin round the streets of Tokyo or disappear into online worlds within worlds. But I don't really want to watch any of them.

I want to be with Rowan. He doesn't just let me watch – he reaches through the screen and takes my hand and it feels electric. He makes me feel like here, in this room, my choices matter.

And now I've ruined it.

I can't entirely remember what I said to him on the stream last time – just that I was angry. Angry at myself for stopping Mum and Dad having lives, and angry with Jonah for stopping Rowan's.

But anger has never been any sort of way to get things done. With Mum and Dad, I smile and tell them I'm fine as much as I can, so they don't have to carry the full weight of the Illness. And to really help Rowan I should have tried a softer approach, too. But it's too late now. He's just another streamer gone.

I am safe. I am happy. I am alive.

I shut my laptop.

36

Alice

Dad has the day off work. He brings me lunch to celebrate, and I do a terrible job of smiling and pretending everything's fine.

He sits on the bed. Holds my hand.

'Tell me,' he says. 'Come on – I want angsty teenager Alice. Give me all your woes.'

I sit up a little. 'It's nothing,' I say. 'I'm feeling better now.'

Dad gives me a look, like he doesn't believe me. 'You know, you can feel better and still be a bit pissed off at the world.'

I laugh, but he doesn't stop staring me down. 'I suppose I'm just wishing I was normal,' I sigh.

'Crikey, things must be bad. Being normal is the worst possible thing you could be.'

I roll my eyes at him.

'I'm serious! Imagine if you were a normal teenager, wearing black and listening to that stuff they call music now. Sorry, kiddo, but I don't think we could be friends if you were normal. Wouldn't be seen dead.'

'You know what I mean,' I say softly and he squeezes my hand.

'What's brought all this on, eh? You've been lying there looking like you were on drugs this past week – I was going to make your mum check for needles.'

I consider telling him about Rowan, but his name isn't for Dad to hear. He's mine. At least he was.

'It's Cecelia,' I say. 'She's been ignoring me since she found out about the Illness.'

'I thought we hadn't had as many break-ins recently.' I give him a look and he smiles. 'I hadn't realized your Illness was a secret.'

I shift. 'Well, it isn't really. But I wanted to forget it for a while, I suppose.'

'Look, kiddo – if Cecelia is the person I think she is, she's not going anywhere. Her mum doesn't allow Pop-Tarts in the house, for one. And if she does run off because of a stupid thing like that, then you don't want her around anyway.'

I nod and smile again, but I don't quite believe him. It's enough to convince him to leave me alone with my lunch, though, and get back to the rugby.

I lie back and close my eyes, trying to disappear into a memory. Of swimming in a lido filled with sun-warmed water, on holiday, until the lifeguard blows her whistle and –

Of being up a tree, climbing so high I feel like I might sprout wings and take off, until I slip and –

Of being on a bike, cycling fast downhill and seeing the world in bloom. But then that car –

I pick up my laptop.

Welcome back to Stream Cast, Alice

Users online:

No one is online yet – why not <u>try making your profile public</u> to connect to more people?

Users offline:

tokyo--drifter	**destroy_roy**	**_1mp0ssibledream_**
Last online:	Last online:	Last online:
7 hours	12 hours	1 day

Rowan	**WesleyCycles67**	**daddycool-007**
Last online:	Last online:	Last online:
11 days	50 days	100 days

Connect to a channel to start watching.

No one's online. Someone is usually always online. Day and night. Even at weekends there's usually a window for me to peer through. But not at the moment. Perhaps they all got bored of streaming, with me not watching them as much.

Stream Cast wants me to go public. I've only ever used it as a private site, with my own streamers who are vetted by my parents, but I know there's a whole other world out there filled with strangers with cameras pointed at goodness knows what. And that's a world that's always scared me, because you just don't know whose life you might stumble into, what you might see, or hear, that will make the bad thoughts tumble in. But perhaps I could just take a peek. Open the window a crack . . .

My mouse is hovering over the 'go live' link when suddenly Rowan's name pops up.

Rowan

Online for 1 minute

I let out my breath all at once, because he's back. He's here, opening a window and letting me climb through. I take a deep breath and clear my throat.

I'll be careful this time. I won't let the Illness overcome me again. I'll hide it much better this time and then – then – maybe he'll stay. Even if Cecelia won't.

Connecting to **Rowan** . . .

37

Rowan

And now I am sitting in the castle climbing frame looking out at bright blue sky that stretches all the way down to a turquoise sea.

Rowan's trainers are up on the mermaid's hands, like she reached out and grabbed him.

'I'm sorry,' I say.

Alice.
My guts do that weird thing
like when you're on a roller coaster and you
d r o p.
'No, I'm sorry.
I'm such a snowflake.
You were only being nice.'

'No! I wasn't listening – I was . . .'

I search for the best words not to give myself away.

'I wasn't thinking straight.'

'Yeah, well, that makes two of us.
So we're okay?'

I sigh, feeling my chest untighten enough to taste the air again.

'Yes. Yes, we're okay.'

> *I look out of the window.*
> *See the plastic bags rolling over the grass*
> *– the dog taking a dump in the sandpit*
> *– and I search for the line of sea in the distance.*
> *'Listen, what I said before about Jonah . . .*
> *I was being overdramatic.*
> *It's just babysitting really.'*

I think back to the texts I've been sending Cecelia about me having the flu, and wonder if he realizes just how similar our lies sound.

'Why did she leave? Your mum.'

> *I swallow.*
> *There's no hiding from this one.*
> *I hang my head back so all I see is*
> *SKY.*
> *'Mam – she's an alcoholic.*
> *She started leaving for weeks at a time,*
> *then one day she . . .*
> *she just didn't come back.'*
> *I can see the top of the bell tower from here.*

At home, I look out of the window and wonder if he's seeing the same perfect stretch of blue sky.

'Didn't you call the police?'

> *I laugh,*
> *but it ain't funny.*
> *'What – and have them*
> *take Jonah away?'*
> *I shake my head.*
> *'I'm not running out on him, too, Alice.'*
> *I'm not failing him*
> *like I failed her.*

I pinch my lips together, because I don't want him to disconnect the stream again. Not when the world is stretched out and waiting for me to leave my footprints in it.

> *'You won't tell anyone, though,*
> *will you?'*

I think of the agreement I made with Mum when she asked me to be her spy on the inside. And now I know what it is that's holding Rowan back. But I suppose she doesn't need to know. I can help him for her.

'I won't say anything. But have you thought about telling anyone else?'

> *I hear laughter coming out of the tunnel down the hill.*
> *Fran and Charlie,*
> *hands in each other's back pockets.*
> *'What, like those bozos?'*

They both have purple streaks today, like they've been swirled in the same pot of paint.

The girl – Fran – waves.

'Ro!' she calls. 'Ro – come down. Charlie's sneaked a slug of his stepdad's finest.'

> *Charlie waves a water bottle half full of*
> *whiskey.*
> *I can still smell it.*
> *On her breath as she said she was sorry – sorry – sorry.*
> *On the carpet as I scrubbed at the stains.*
> *On Jonah's pillow and school clothes and socks.*
> *'I'm good!' I shout over.*

Fran throws her arms up. 'Come on, dude. Don't be boring. Lunch is nearly over.'

> *I keep my eyes*
> *on the sky.*

'Are they always like that – your friends?' I ask as they give up and disappear down the path.

> *'They are now, yeah.*
> *Didn't use to be, though.*
> *We used to hang out a lot.*
> *We met in, like, Year One or something,*
> *bonded over finger-painting.*
> *Charlie's not really as into art any more,*

but Fran is.
She even helped me out with the kraken.
But then they got together and –'

'– love turned them gross,' I say, thinking of what Cecelia said when we watched that film.

I laugh.
'Yeah. Something like that.'
The line of sea in the distance glitters.
'How about you, Alice? You gross?'

I'm not sure what he's asking. But the words make my throat dry and my face crack a smile.

'I could be,' I whisper.

38

Alice

It's Wednesday night again and, instead of some strange cure that Dad plucks from his mind, we're doing something that might actually be useful.

We're talking to my cardiologist.

She's my favourite specialist. Not because she's nice – Dad was right when he said that she has 'the social skills of a pineapple' – but because she listens to me and believes that the Illness is real.

'This beats the commute, eh?' Dad says, wheeling the desk chair over to my bed as Mum sets up the chat on my laptop.

Travelling to see my cardiologist = more spoons than I have

Dad's right. It's so much better this way. Dr Rahman is based all the way in north London. I haven't seen her in about a year, because last time it took enough spoons to leave me with weeks of fog. But now I don't need to battle with the spoon-annihilating noise and the flashing lights and the earthquake that is the car. I can do it all from my bed via video link.

It's strange that Mum is on my laptop, though, and she keeps batting my hand away as the cursor comes dangerously close to opening screenshots I've taken of Rowan and Me Living.

'Alice! For Christ's sake – just let me do this, okay? For someone who's always on that bloody Stream Cast, you'd think you'd have your webcam set up.'

I sit back and sigh. 'You know that's not how it works.'

Imagine what Rowan would see if it were the other way round. A pillow. A duvet. A ghost girl.

She finally manages to get it set up and puts the laptop on a pile of books at the foot of the bed before scrambling up next to me. And I can see us – all of us – squished in a line together on my bed. Watching. And it's strange to look at this housebound family in another place, until we shrink to the square in the bottom corner and Dr Rahman's face fills the screen instead.

It makes me jump, seeing her on my laptop. Because it's not like a usual streamer, where I can trick myself into thinking that I'm there with them. It's like she's jumped from London and appeared here, inside my bedroom.

'H-hello!' Dad shouts, bending awkwardly and waving over my face. 'Can you hear us, Dr Rahman?'

'We're-so-glad-you-could-fit-us-in,' Mum says, like she's speaking to someone who lip-reads.

I sink down a little bit as Dr Rahman pauses, looking at her notes.

'Yes. Alice, tell me about this episode the other week. Your notes here say that your blood pressure dropped to eighty over forty?'

And that's the other thing I like about Dr Rahman. She doesn't speak to Mum or Dad. She speaks to me.

I tell her about the dropped spoons and the breathlessness, and I show her the recorded results on my heart monitor. And she asks questions, all the time writing, writing. And I tell her in as much detail as I can remember.

Video consultation = 3 spoons

When the fifteen minutes are up, she looks at her notes for a moment in silence and it feels like we're watching a reality show where the host pauses before delivering the news that someone is going home.

'I want to try you on some blood-volume enhancers. See how you get on.'

And we thank her for her time, shut down the video link and close my laptop before we celebrate. Because she listened. She heard. And she gave us something that's worth a hundred more sessions like that one.

Hope.

39

Rowan

And now I am strapped to the chest of a boy who's just finished work. We planned it this way.

'Run,' I say.

> *What is it with this girl*
> *and running?*
> *'Where to?'*

'Anywhere.' I look at the steps leading up to the busy road, cars thundering over the tunnel we found before. 'Along the beach. As far as it goes.'

> *I look at my watch.*
> *'I've got to pick Jonah up in half an hour.'*
> *But I do it. I run.*

And I can hear the thud of his body working. His bones as he skids on stones. His lungs as he sucks in the world and his veins as he pumps it round his body.

And somehow it makes me feel close to Cecelia.

> *Running is horrible.*
> *Air stabs in my chest.*
> *A stitch claws at my ribs.*
> *But also.*
> *I feel sort of*
> *A L I V E.*

The world rocks from side to side and in it I see people walking blurs of dogs, elderly couples browsing souvenir shops, hand in hand, a huge ship stalking the horizon.

And then that sound starts to buzz again.

> *For a moment,*
> *I think I'm having a heart attack.*
> *Then I realize it's just the phone on my chest.*
> *I stop, stooping to look at the caller ID.*

I see a whisper of his hair – long and dark – and it sends a charge through my shoulders.

The buzzing stops. 'Another call?'

> *I pant like a dog*
> *and crawl to a bench.*
> *'Just my dad again.'*
> *Sitting feels*
> *miraculous.*

'Oh – but you said he left?'

'Yeah.
Exactly.
He left, but he keeps calling,
like that makes it okay.'

'Maybe calling is all he can do . . .' I say, looking at my feet trapped under the duvet.

'He's in Australia, so, yeah.
It was his choice to go, though.
He got some opportunity at work and just –
left.
Even with Mam being –'
I look out to sea,
where a bloke is skipping stones with a kid
about Jonah's age.
'Anyway. What are your folks like?
Your mam's the careers lady, yeah?'

I clench my fists, thinking carefully.
 'My mum works at the school, yes. And my dad's in IT.'

'Any brothers or sisters?'

'No – just me.' I try to say it cheerily. Although sometimes I wonder what it would be like to have another kid trapped inside this family with me.

The bloke and kid I'm watching
chase each other,
up and down the beach.
'Seems like a pretty sweet deal.'

I bite my lip. Because here he is again, making assumptions about me and my life, with no idea –

But that's what I want, isn't it? That's what will make him stay.

'It's not all roses, you know. Being . . . home-schooled. It gets lonely.'

I look at my shoes.
'Why don't you come out here, then?
Come running.'

My heart is beating like I already am out there.

'I can't do that,' I say quickly. 'Anyway, you're Living for me, remember? Our project?'

I hear it in her voice.
Ghost girl's got a secret.
I want to ask what it is,
like maybe an old witch is keeping her chained up
– or maybe she's allergic to the sun
– or maybe she's just shy or something.
But that's the thing with secrets.
Some are best kept hidden.
'Course,' I say quietly.
'So what do you wanna do next?'

He stands and starts walking back along the beach to pick Jonah up.

'Maybe you could show me more paintings?'

'Is that what you really want to do?
You don't seem like the type to be into graffiti,
with it being illegal and everything.'

I open my mouth and close it again, because I suppose it is. When I think about it, I've perhaps done more illegal things with Rowan than I have my entire life. And that's both exciting and terrifying.

'What do you like to do?
Art? Music?
BDSM?'

He says it in the present tense. I almost forget to tut at him.

'I used to like to cycle.'

'Really?'

I think about it and actually – no – *I* didn't. I liked it well enough when I was streaming with Wes– I shake my head again.

But back when I could ride my bike, I spent more time going down mountains than I did on the roads. And even then I was only doing it because Dad was.

If it were up to me, I'd be spending all my time underwater.

As he walks, I see a building emerge beside us, standing tall in the middle of the traffic on the road above, like a castle with a moat.

'The Aquatic Centre,' I breathe.

I slip my hands into my empty pockets.
'Ain't that just for little kids?'

'No!' I say, ignoring all the children pointing at the sharks on the billboards around the sides.

I remember coming here before. Dad took me on one of our adventure days. I remember feeling as though I were under the water, swimming through coral reefs and following fish on their circuits. It was what started my swimming lessons. What started me thinking that I might want to be a marine biologist one day.

It's what started Me.

Rowan's quiet and I see the prices listed on the side.

'I'll buy the ticket online tonight,' I say. 'We can go tomorrow.'

Tomorrow.
I could probably bunk off school again.
Let's be honest –
only Jonah would notice if I
d i s a p p e a r e d.

Rowan steps up off the beach and starts walking to the road, to where the cars thunder.

My finger hovers over the disconnect button.

> *'Okay, ghost girl.*
> *Tomorrow it is.'*

40

Alice

It's movie night and Cecelia isn't here. But Mum is.

We're watching something Cecelia would probably be calling 'old-person porn', about a woman who falls in love with someone she shouldn't. And Mum is sharing far too many details about her 'youth' that I really don't need to know about.

If I'm honest, I'm missing Cecelia. However much Mum tries, her 'girl talk' isn't quite the same.

The credits roll and she sinks down to face me so we're sharing the same pillow. She smells like face cream and that smells like home.

She smiles and raises her eyebrows. 'So . . . how's your spy mission with Rowan going?'

My stomach backflips. 'Fine,' I say quickly, sitting up so she can't stare at me.

She pokes my ribs. 'I thought that might get your attention.'

I shake her off. 'No . . . it's not like that. I just – the streamers are mine. I don't like –'

'Yes, I know you don't like sharing all your adventures with your boring old mum.' She sits up next to me. 'But we had a deal, remember? You were going to be my spy on the inside. Wesley –'

My throat dries and I cough over her words so she has to stop and smack me on the back.

I take a deep breath. And pick my words carefully.

'Yes. Rowan showed me what's going on with him and it's nothing bad!' I say quickly as she opens her mouth. 'And I think – I think I can get through to him. He just needs a bit more time.'

Mum smiles and takes my hand. 'I have no doubt that you will. But you know he's been missing a lot of classes recently. He was supposed to see me for a review session just the other day and he didn't turn up. And you've been dropping more spoons than usual, too. So –'

I shake her off again. 'Oh, that's nothing. I'm not even with him that much. The other streamers are –'

'Wondering where you've got to, yes,' Mum says, loving this a little too much.

I turn my head away so she can't see me die.

She laughs. 'It's okay, Alice. I'm just saying, be careful. For both of you. And, you know, if you're going to fall in *lurve* with him –'

I choke. 'I am *not* –'

But she's really laughing now. Laughing more than I've seen her laugh in ages and ages, wrestling my hands back as I try to push her away. And then. Then she starts singing.

It's an old Spice Girls' song. And she's singing it entirely to tick me off and it's working. But her voice in my room feels like a bright white light, warm on my face.

She sings. Even when I drop a spoon to throw a pillow at her, and even when she laughs so hard she almost falls off the bed, she keeps on singing. And when she gets to the chorus at the end, I do my best to sing the in-between notes usually reserved for Fake Mel C, and it sounds like something is dying in my throat.

The song ends and she flops back on to my pillow. 'How did my daughter end up with a voice like that? You must've got it from your dad – he couldn't carry a tune in a wheelbarrow, either.'

I tut at her. 'Well, we can't all be as perfect as you.'

We get our breath back as the light leaks out of the sky outside, and the music seems to disappear with it. I watch the last of the sun swirling round the ceiling like water disappearing down a drain.

'Do you miss it? Singing,' I whisper.

I feel her breathing freeze. Just for a moment. Then she smiles. 'Nah. Touring was the worst – they always put us in the most awful hotels. I tell you, the real Vicky Beckham wouldn't have stood for it.'

She laughs, but it doesn't quite cover the sadness sitting on the back of her tongue. It doesn't quite cover the lie.

She heaves herself up, shutting off the TV and picking up our dinner plates.

It's a different kind of dance to the one she used to do, but it's just as graceful. Just as practised and refined.

She bends down to kiss me on the head.

'You okay?' she asks.

And I may not be able to sing, but I can do these moves with her, perfectly synchronized.

'I'm wonderful,' I smile.

41

Rowan

And now I am with someone who's waiting outside the Aquatic Centre for me like I'm actually joining him there – not just via the internet. And there's something lovely about that, especially as the wind is so strong that it's whipping the sea over cars in the car park.

If I weren't strapped to his chest, I'd run up to him. Hang off his arm.

'Hi,' I say instead.

> *Finally,*
> *she's online.*
> *'Shall we go in?'*
> *I shout over the wind.*

He doesn't wait for an answer and I'm pleased. We step between the glass doors and dive into a world of unopened post and cardboard boxes, a plastic shark hanging from the ceiling with its nose missing, and I can't help but think –

I'm home.

I've never seen such a dump.
'It's a tenner to come in here?'
For that, I could
feed Jonah and me for
two whole days.

'Just you wait.'

A girl with a ring through her nose smiles glumly
as I show her the ticket Alice forwarded me.
It's weird —
the ticket is just for one,
but it feels like it's for
both of us.

'First feed's in fifteen minutes,' she says in a bored voice.

Rowan thanks her and I hold my breath as we walk through the black-flap door, because I'm finally doing it. I'm not cycling, or playing games, practising kicks, or wandering round the streets of Tokyo. I'm Living my own life and I'm choosing to dive.

Well, here goes nothing.
But I hope —
for Alice's sake —
that it's at least something.

We pass through to the other side and the lighting is dim. The world blurs and warps as the camera struggles to cling on to what is real. The sound of drowning and the distant screaming of children and the whirring of machines keeping things alive roars though the microphone all at once and I choke on it.

But then the bubbles clear and we're gliding across a seabed, red and green light bulbs making everything feel as if we've passed into another world. Rock walls tumble into a long corridor, with tanks on every side, brightly lit and swimming with life, like little pockets of sea.

> *Ghost girl*
> *has disappeared on me again.*
> *'You okay?'*

And I mean it this time. 'I'm wonderful.'

Rowan chuckles and bends down at the first tank, open at the top and glass from the waist down. We watch as huge silver fish bump and nudge each other along, eyes following us as we crawl round the outside, peering in at them.

> *It's like watching an underwater rush hour.*
> *'Do you reckon they think we're*
> *in the tank with them?'*

'We are!'

Mum closed the curtains in my room before she left this morning, shrinking my room down to one window at the very bottom of the sea. And I can feel the water between my fingers. Feel the slippery bumps as the fish tumble against me in a mad dash to get to the edge of the glass, only to turn and dive back round again.

We make our way to the next tank. This one is filled with small tropical fish. They swim in different directions, oranges, blues, yellows and golds colliding.

'They're like confetti.'

> *This tank looks like that film*
> *Jonah loves.*
> *'Hey, look –*
> *I found Nemo.'*

'A clownfish. They're always everyone's favourite.'

> *Favourite*
> *is a pretty strong word for a fish.*
> *'All right, so here's a question.*
> *What would you be,*
> *if you were a fish?'*

I think about that for a moment. 'A mudskipper. They can live in water, but they can also hop across land.'

And I like the idea of that. That my body might be stuck blowing bubbles, but I'm free to run and breathe.

> *'Um, I'm pretty sure fish don't walk, Alice.'*

'Some do! In fact – there – check out that one on the bottom.'

We watch as a fish that looks as if the whole Earth has been swirled together and moulded into fish form scuttles across the bottom of the tank like a crab playing dress-up.

'Well – shit.
Would you look at that?
How d'you know this stuff?'

'I told you – I watch a lot of documentaries. I'm hoping to be a marine biologist one day.'
One day.
One day.

'Smart.
I duck down and read the sign.
'Mandarin fish do not have scales
but are covered in a bitter slime
to repel predators.'

'Hey!' I say as he dissolves into laughter. 'I'm a mudskipper, anyway – that's not the same as this one.'

'Whatever you say.
Mud –
slime –
all the same, if you ask me.'

I tut at him as we walk further down the corridor to where a huge open tank sits in a corner, bubbling over with bream, sharks and –

> *'Oh cool – rays.'*
> *They're swimming around in this*
> *big open bath*
> *that smells like rotten sea monkeys.*

And I can probably forgive him for calling me slimy when he says a thing like that. Because rays are magnificent. My favourite documentary has a whole episode about them. And from it I know that rays don't have a single bone in their whole body. And that some have even been known to jump up out of the water and fly like birds.

We watch as one flutters up from the floor of the tank, ribboning as it pokes its nose up to the surface, showing us the cut-out mask of a face hidden underneath.

'A sea ghost.'

> *I stand closer to the tank.*
> *'How d'you come up with stuff like that?*
> *I was just gonna say that rays*
> *look a lot weirder from underneath,*
> *but you . . .*
> *It's like you see this whole other world.'*

'I don't know . . . I suppose it's the same as when you paint, isn't it? Just another way of splashing a bit of colour on the world.'

We watch the ray ripple over sharks as they barb left and right, and between bream as they swim round and round. But his words have made me feel like I've swum through a thermal.

Children seem to descend from nowhere and Rowan moves to let a small boy go in front of him. It's a nice thing to do, but I can't help but be a bit annoyed that we can't see as well any more.

A man in an Aquatic Centre shirt quietens the crowd, holding a large tub to his chest.

> *This guy looks a bit more enthusiastic*
> *than the girl at reception did.*
> *But then again,*
> *he's holding a bucket of fish guts.*

'Okay, I'm gonna be chucking this in now, so you kids are probably gonna want to take a step back – first few rows might get wet.'

Everyone shuffles back except the boy Rowan let in front of him, who keeps his hands and face pressed against the glass.

> *I look for the kid's mam and*
> *she's got her head down.*
> *Playing some game on her phone.*
> *If Alice wasn't here watching,*
> *I'd probably say something*
> *I shouldn't.*

The man tips his tub into the water and the tank comes to life. The water boils as silver-foil shapes swish and teeth tear. And the little boy at the front screams as water splashes out of the tank and drenches him, plastering his hair to his head.

He turns, face twisted in a way that looks like he might cry. I brace myself for the noise to cut me.

I run forward and
duck down next to the kid,
pointing at the tank.
'Look!
That ray has a squid in its mouth.'

The boy and I watch wide-eyed as the ray circles, tentacles rolling from its hidden jaws.

'He's going to eat it!' the boy shouts a bit pointlessly, as we can already see that for ourselves. The ray does a victory lap of the tank, then flips, white side up, and starts sucking the rest into its mouth like spaghetti.

'Cool!' the boy says, but I think I feel slightly sick.

We stand back as more people arrive and we slip round a corner into a deserted corridor.

'So you're a seahorse?' I say.

We watch one in the tank opposite us, its tail wrapped tightly round a piece of weed.

'Seahorse?
I'm way cooler than a seahorse.'

'Seahorses are cool. It's the males that give birth, you know . . .'

> *She's talking about that kid and*
> *about Jonah, too.*
> *'I look after Jonah,*
> *but, you know, he's not*
> *all I am.'*
> *I feel like*
> *utter shit*
> *for even saying that.*

My heart soars like a flying fish.
'So tell me. Who are you?'

> *'I dunno.'*
> *Seems like a big question for*
> *such a quiet space.*
> *'I'm nothing like a seahorse, though.*
> *I'd want to be something awesome,*
> *like your walking fish or whatever.'*

We walk slowly by tanks with crabs and lobsters in them, like counters at a supermarket.
And then I see it. Rowan. In fish form.
'Stop! That's it.'

> *We bend to peer in*
> *at this bug-eyed purple shrimp*
> *half buried in a*

fake seabed.
'You think I'm a prawn?'
Great.
Way to make an impression there.

'Read the sign.'

I stand and read.
'"Mantis shrimps can see
TEN TIMES
as many colours as humans.
Their punch is as forceful
as a twenty-two-calibre bullet
and fifty times faster
than the blink of an eye.
Their limbs cause bubbles to collapse as
micro-implosions in the water
that reach temperatures close to
the surface of the sun."
Um . . .'
We bend down again
to look at the puny shrimp.
'That little thing
can do all that?'

I smile. 'I told you the sea is full of wonders.'

She says it like she thinks
maybe I can be that, too.

I look up at a sign above the door next to us.
'I want to try something.
Something like
"wonderful".'

My breath quickens and I'm not sure why.
 'Okay . . .'

'I'm gonna cut the stream for a bit, okay?'

'Oh . . .'

She doesn't like that idea,
but she will when she sees.
'Only for a moment.
I want to show you something
and it'll be more impressive
if you just tune in when it's happening.
And maybe –
maybe imagine that you really are
M E.'
Someone a ghost girl
thinks could be wonderful.

I grumble, wondering about all the Living I'll be missing in
those moments that he's gone. But he takes it as a yes, and I
see his thumb reaching up before the screen goes black.

Rowan is no longer streaming.

42

Alice

I'm spat back into my bed again and I feel sick. And that means that I should stop the stream now and get some rest.

I swallow. Close my eyes.

Rowan's asked me to imagine that I'm him. Not as a watcher, or even as a 'we'. As an 'I'. And I want to be an 'I' in a body that can crouch down to watch rays and then race down corridors and then – well. Do whatever it is that he's about to do. Something wonderful.

But I remember what happened last time I lost track of my spoons. And Mum's right – I do need to be careful.

Going to the Aquatic Centre with Rowan = 3 spoons

I grip the laptop like a float and hope it's enough to keep me on the surface. Just for a moment longer. Just for this. Please.

I see Rowan switch from offline to online. And I click before my shaking hands become hands that don't move at all.

Connecting to **Rowan** . . .

43

~~Rowan~~ Me

And now I am . . . I am underwater.

And I'm not Rowan.

I am Me.

I am lying on the seabed, looking up at a bright light that's like the sun. The light refracts as the water waves, making it seem as though white flames are burning the edges of my eyes.

And above me. Around me. Everywhere. Are fish. Fish of all colours. Of all types.

A small shoal of flatfish with yellow tails paddle over to my left, each one reluctant to take charge of where the rest are going. In the distance, smaller, brighter fish swim in and out of coral, some attached to the tops of big silver fish with fat lips. Another comes flying out of nowhere, fins flapping like wings as it soars over my head and out of sight.

And then a blue-tipped shark. Strong arrow tail propelling the rest of it forward, left, right, like a soldier marching.

My lungs putter out of air and I gasp a mouthful of water. But I must have gills, because I'm breathing. Finally. Breathing.

Or perhaps I am a mudskipper after all. A fish with legs. I am land and sea and mountains and fire. I am unstoppable. Unbreakable. And I put out my hand and watch as my long fingers drift through the water. Feel it flutter. Watch as my skin becomes transparent and peels away to reveal silver scales underneath.

And then I'm floating Up Towards the surface. And I can see it, where the light is and the bubbles break, and I hold my breath so the taste is all the sweeter. I stretch my hands out further and can almost feel the edge – the line between water and air – like I might be able to grab hold of it and pull it back and reveal a whole world of in-between, where a fish can Live in both at once.

But I'm not quite there. Not quite. So instead I turn. Pirouetting like a dolphin until I'm not looking at the light any more. But there aren't any jagged rocks, either. Instead, I'm looking at a boy lying on the floor of an aquarium tunnel, watching me as I swim overhead, his long dark hair fanned out under him. He looks at me and I wonder if his eyes are almost entirely black, until I see the glittering somewhere in the middle, where the light reflected from the top can make gems out of the hardest of stones.

For one suspended moment, I look at him like he's just another fish. Powerful. Colourful.

Beautiful.

But then I come to my senses in a way that feels like
sinking
because
this boy
this boy is Rowan.

44

Alice

I wake up to humming and see that Mum's brought me some pink tulips from the garden, still cupped like dancer's feet. I smile and she sees.

'Good dream?'

She takes the vase from my window and fills it with water from the bathroom sink.

'I've been swimming,' I say, watching the ceiling swirl.

I fell asleep almost the moment I disconnected from Rowan and it was like my head never really left. All night, I replayed the moment I turned and saw his face as he lay on the dusty floor of the aquarium tunnel and fish swam above.

This morning, I feel almost weightless.

Mum pushes my window open and the sounds of kids getting dropped off at school swim over my head. Usually the laughing and the footsteps hammering on the pavement outside is a ray with a sting. But today a group of girls chattering are brightly coloured angelfish. A woman shouting at someone to slow down is a turtle with long, sweeping feet. And the sound of my own mum, humming to herself, is like a strawberry anemone unfurling from the sides of my tank.

He doesn't look anything like I thought he would.

Whenever I think of boys, I picture them with short hair and dirt smeared over their cheeks. I suppose that's what they looked like when I was last at school. They all had grass-stained knees and fingers up their noses and were generally unpleasant to be around.

But Rowan has long hair – chestnut brown – that was fanning out all around him on the floor, like he really was at the bottom of the sea. He looked clean, too, with a square jaw and eyes like dark stones. And I think about what he might look like next to me and my stomach flips like a fish out of water.

And it's strange. Because, however much I wanted to take over his body and become him in that moment, seeing his face has made me want something else even more. I want to be with him. Beside him. Holding his hand and looking at the same world together – as similar but impossibly different people.

I'm blushing as Mum bends down to pop headphones over my ears, and I hope she can't reach down and see into the bottom of my thoughts. I don't have the energy to smack her with a pillow again.

Faraway music starts playing through my headphones and I feel like I might be pinned to a violin. I watch her turn on the vacuum cleaner and push it round the carpet, only hearing a light buzz.

I stretch my eyes to the window, where I can see the school in the shadow of the bell tower. But somewhere down there, among the parents and the children, is Rowan – dropping his little brother off at school and thinking about heading to his own class.

And even though I don't have the spoons to join him today, he feels close enough now that I might reach out and touch him.

45

Alice

I'm back to a full twelve spoons and, although that means I can just about stumble to the bathroom, I feel like dancing.

Mum and Dad seem different, too. Their foreheads are less creased and I can hear them downstairs, laughing. And even though I have no idea what could be so funny, I smile at myself in the mirror and look almost back to pre-Illness Alice – just for one snapshot.

I wander back to bed and stretch my toes, pushing my hands under my pillows as far as they'll go, like an athlete limbering up. Then something catches my knuckle – something spiky and flat.

I pick it out. It's a pink sequin star. For a moment, I'm so trapped in my own good mood that I pass it off as another of Dad's games. That perhaps he's found a way to bring a whole night sky into my bedroom. But then I remember. And it feels like sinking in a thick green pond.

Cecelia.

She was wearing a crown of these the night everything went wrong. I remember her throwing it from her head where it exploded against my wall, raining a whole sky of regret on to me.

I can feel the edges of the star now like they're caught between my ribs, next to the jagged piece of camera lens I carry for Wes–

I don't want to forget her like I forget him, though. I don't want to push her down and ignore her and pretend she didn't happen. I want to cling to the hope that she'll come charging back through my bedroom door with a whole new colour in her braids, calling everything ancient history.

But the more I cling to this star, the more the edges push into my skin.

Mum kicks open the bedroom door and I jolt back to life.

'You okay, sweetheart?' she says as she tops up my med box with the day's pills.

I push the star back under my pillow, as far as it'll go, and smile at her. 'Yes, I'm fine. What was so funny downstairs?'

Mum's too busy laughing again to see the folds at the corners of my smile. She tells me a story about Dad putting ketchup on his porridge instead of jam and I laugh along with her in all the right places.

I only have three hours until I'm back with Rowan again. And in that time, I say goodbye to Mum and Dad as they head off to work, and watch the flowers on my window sill bloom over the noise of people getting up and going to school and work and Living their whole wide lives.

Meanwhile, I watch my old documentaries – trying to pretend I'm living in a blue-green world with microscopic shrimps next door to ancient turtles. And I see some of the fish that swam above me when I last saw Rowan, living out in the wild and going wherever they want to go.

Then, when waiting feels like algae bubbles glugging up my windpipe, I open my laptop.

Connecting to **Rowan** . . .

46

Rowan

And now I am back behind a long, paint-splattered desk, looking out on a classroom of people talking loudly, throwing bits of clay and ripping up paper.

I eye the walls, looking for hints of Wesley again, but finding only colour and sculptures and life.

'It's very loud in here today!' I shout.

She's back.
Ghost girl's alive again.
YOU OKAY? *I write in my sketchbook.*
FISH TUNNEL A BAD IDEA?
Honestly,
you show a girl what you look like
and she logs off for days.
Nothing like that to get you
STARING
into the mirror.

'No, not at all – it was wonderful. I just – I had to go. But it really was the best day.'

I should feel relieved,
but I feel something else.
Something anxious –
tight –
but also sort of amazing.
SORRY, CAN'T TALK PROPERLY.

'That's okay. What's the lesson on today?'

Charlie kicks me under the table
to show me the boobs he's carved into the desk.
NOTHING – FREE DRAWING AGAIN.
I roll my eyes at him.

'Does that mean you're free to do anything you want?'

I look around to see what other people are doing. Some are creating collages out of tissue paper, ribbons twirling together to create plaited rainbows. Someone at the back is building what looks like a castle from purple playdough, complete with a glitter moat.

And there're Rowan's friends again. Both dressed today in rainbows, almost like it's their personal couple's uniform. It seems like a whole world away from Rowan's grey sweatshirt, even though they're sitting right next to each other. Their hands are wrapped together as they bend over their desks and scribble.

'So, Rowan, what are you going to draw?'

I shrug, but pull the pot of
black ink towards me.

'Must be nice,' I say quickly, 'to have a whole hour just to be free. I suppose you could be anything you wanted to be, in whatever form you pleased. You could be on land or sea, or in between and both.'

> *My pen hovers above the page.*
> *I hadn't really thought about the*
> *F R E E part*
> *of free drawing.*
> *And here's Alice again.*
> *Making me feel like I could*
> *– draw*
> *– do*
> *– be*
> *anything.*

I watch as he drops his pen and picks up a pencil.

He sketches with scattered lines at first, like he's unsure of what he's drawing. But then his hand rests on the page and his lines become darker – surer. And, out from the blank page, eyes open.

The drawings seem to dance round each other, the figure at the bottom playing the maracas while the one at the top pirouettes through the air, as if gravity couldn't possibly hold it down. And then, as his lines quicken, he drops his pencil.

He picks up a paintbrush and he dips it in blue.

> *I'm not thinking about her –*
> *Mam –*

because it's different this time.
I'm not forcing colour into the
dregs of a hangover.
I'm not painting to
– cheer her up, or
– try to stop her drinking again, or
– make her stay this time.
I'm choosing colour because
with Alice
it's there.

He paints over the grey of the pencil, flicking colour outside the lines and sweeping it across the page, turning snow to sea.

He flecks it across the body at the top and blends it to an oil-spill rainbow of colour in the body at the bottom. And as he adds reds and oranges and greens and purples, I realize what it is he's painting.

It's a mantis shrimp. Out of his seabed hideaway, his eyes looking up at the clouds as a great blue-spotted mudskipper leaps overhead, fins out wide like wings.

It's him. And me. Bursting from the same page in full technicolour.

My throat feels dry. 'You looked up mudskippers.'

I put down my paintbrush and look at
my paint-flecked hands.
'Turns out there are

thirty-two different species of mudskipper.
But this one.
The blue one.
This felt the most like you.'

He says it out loud and Charlie uncurls himself from Fran. He looks at Rowan's page and elbows her in the ribs.

'Ow!' she says, jumping up. 'What you –'

But then she sees. They both do. And they look at the space where I know Rowan's face is and I feel jealousy charge through my bones like electricity.

'Nice fish, dude,' Fran says quietly.

They're looking at me like I'm mad.
Like I'm three-years-ago Rowan.

'You wanna come hang at the bell tower later?' Charlie says, still looking at Rowan's painting. 'Fran reckons we can bust open the fire door. It'll be like old times.'

The bell goes and everyone
JUMPS UP
along with my insides.
I check my watch.
'Jonah,' I mutter.

Fran rolls her eyes and turns away. 'You babysit way too much.'

189

I look at the painting one last time.
Then I screw it up
and throw it in the bin on my way out.

Rowan is no longer streaming.

47

Alice

Dad sticks his head round the door. 'Oi, you. Spoon count?'

I frown. 'But it's not Wednesday?'

He exaggerates a sigh. 'Can't a guy do something fun any other day of the week? Spoon count.'

I smile. 'Six?'

'Good enough.'

He pushes open the door and I see he's wearing an apron with a golden 'M' on it. Behind him, Mum's holding a huge tray – so large that she can't reach her arms completely round it to wedge it through the door.

'Have you been to McDonald's?!' I say, my heart dropping a little bit.

'No, no.' Dad puts his finger in the air. 'McDonald's has come to *you*.'

Mum puts the tray down in the middle of the floor and I strain to see what it is, but Dad steps in my way.

'Can I take your order, ma'am?'

Laughing at Dad being ridiculous = 1 spoon

'Ummm . . . Happy Meal, please. Do they still do them?'

I remember we'd go after swimming practice sometimes, pulling in at the drive-through and ordering a Happy Meal each – even Mum and Dad. And we'd bring them home and have a picnic on the living-room floor, swapping toys and gherkins and milkshakes.

'Of course they still do Happy Meals – they're an institution,' Mum says.

Dad steps back as she brings me over a box painted yellow and red, and something in a paper cup with a plastic lid.

I look up at them. 'But I can't eat –'

'Just open it,' Dad says, bringing two other boxes on to the bed for him and Mum.

I pull the handles and inside is a wrapped burger and a chip box, exactly as I remember them . . . but not quite.

I pull out the chips and laugh. 'Cucumber chips! My favourite.'

Mum has the same. 'Don't forget the sauce,' she says, balancing three tiny cups of mayonnaise on the duvet.

I take out the burger and unwrap it, slowly. And inside is a burger, without the bun, covered in shredded lettuce and a thick slab of vegan cheese.

'How did you do this?'

Dad takes a bite of his burger – also bunless. 'I went in just to ask for the boxes, but turns out they don't do that. So I bought three Happy Meals, came home and washed all the packaging until it was a no-gluten, no-carb, no-onion, no-whatever-else zone.'

'But what did you do with the real Happy Meals?' I say.

He shrugs, taking another bite. 'I ate them in the car.'

Mum stops eating. 'You ate all three meals?'

'I did,' he says, swallowing.

'And now you're eating that one . . .'

He nods again, but he's smiling this time.

'Greedy sod.' Mum shakes her head.

I take a bite of my burger. And if I close my eyes, it really is just like being nine again, having picnics on the floor. Even though it's cucumber, and special plain burgers Dad has fried himself, and really just the simple food I eat every day – it feels different. Like going back in time.

'Don't forget your toy,' Dad says.

Mum tuts. 'Isn't Alice a bit old for –'

'No way!' I say, scrabbling in the box.

I have a clockwork T-rex that marches across my knee when I wind it up. And I think of Rowan pairing small dinosaur socks and I wonder if – one day – I could give this to his brother. I clutch it.

Mum has a stegosaurus who sings when you press its belly and Dad has a pterodactyl stress toy, which, he says, will come in handy when he's fighting Mum over who does the washing-up.

And when we've finished, we sit up and drink our Diet Cokes and talk and laugh and pretend that we're a real family in a real restaurant. And it makes me feel that little bit more real myself.

'So is Monday night going to be McDonald's night from now on?' I ask Dad.

He pats his belly. 'I don't think I have the stomach for that.'

Mum gathers up all the rubbish and whispers in my ear, 'Looks like he does to me.'

48

Rowan

And now I am walking through town with Rowan, dodging shoppers with heavy bags and people riding skateboards on the pavement.

The streets throb with people, like we're inside the artery of a giant grey heart. We skirt round toddlers who are tied to their parents by reins. We stumble into a bollard to avoid a family with their noses pressed against a restaurant window, looking at a menu. We duck and we dodge and we speed up and we slow down.

'Where are we going?'

'Oh, hey!'
I shout into my earphone mic.
'My boss Sue needs
some money paying into the bank.
Thought you'd like to come for the ride.'
I'm not sure she can see much
with all these tourists infest the place.

It's not at all like Tokyo, and not just because I'm not being helicoptered around. The shopfronts are salt-stained and don't buzz with screens showing worlds within worlds. They're closed off from the street by doors and don't come spilling out into the crowds. I distantly remember parts of it from when I'd go shopping with Mum, but not enough for me to know exactly where I am. It's like walking through the memory of an old dream.

Rowan turns to avoid a kid on a scooter and I can see now why all the people have been pushed to the sides.

In the middle is a valley of cars.

On one side of the road, the cars sit bumper to bumper, chugging out smoke and glinting like silver teeth. The other side is clear until a red sports car thunders up, rattling the shop windows with a guttering roar.

My chest tightens.

'Is there a quieter route?'

I can see the bank at the top of the road. But.
'Sure.'
I duck down a side street.

I still feel like I'm choking.

'Not a fan of people either, eh?'

'It's not the people,' I gasp. 'It's the cars.'

Cars that stop people altogether.

I know there's a car park ahead this way.
So I turn right, down an alley with overflowing bins and
half-stolen bikes and
trainers wrapped round overhead wires.

It's dark. It's dark.

I blink and turn the brightness up on my laptop, but I know this darkness. It's Wesley. Creeping out of the drawer in the back of my mind like a lost shadow. Wesley – who would have died somewhere on one of these roads.

Wesley, whose blood might still be on the tarmac, being run over again and again by cars and cars and cars driven by people who have no idea what's under their wheels. People who weren't there to see it.

Not like I was.

'Can we stop?'

She sounds out of breath.
'Sure.'
I move a snail off a red–brick wall and
sit down in its place.
'You okay?'

I think about making something up again. But I'm losing track of all the lies.

I close my eyes. 'No.'

I kick the wall behind me.
'If I'd known you were afraid of cars,
I'd never have –'

'I'm not afraid,' I say.

I used to love them. I'd sit with my head out of the window like a dog as Dad drove me to our next adventure. I'd push him to go faster – faster – but then I saw what's at the end of a speed record and –

Wrists. Wrists. Where are my wrists?

'Alice?
It's all right, you know.
I'm not a fan of . . .
some stuff, too.'
I hunt the skyline for the
bell tower in the distance.

I unstick my throat.

'Show me something wonderful,' I say. 'Show me something Alive.'

'Alive?'
I can see
seagulls in the sky.
The snail I moved.
A line of ants crawling over a spat-out sweet.
It's all alive, but
it's not particularly wonderful.
'I dunno if this counts . . .'
I get off the wall and
walk back to the mouth of the alley.

I don't want to go back towards the road, and I'm almost ready to scream at him to stop when he does anyway. And he takes the camera off his chest and tilts it so I can see the pavement.

And on the ground, in the middle of an alleyway, is a painting. Dusty and scuffed by shoes, but still there. Colour rolls round the corner of a building ahead, unfurling like a carpet at our feet. Pinks, blues, greens and yellows scratch into one another – droplets of what look like water just about still glistening in the sun overhead.

It's like peering into the top of a snow globe, but I feel like the one who's been shaken.

'Is it one of yours?'

I swallow.
'Yeah. Kind of.'

My breathing is going back to normal.
'What is it?'

Seeing it now,
it looks like nothing.
Like a skidmark from something that
never should have happened.
'It was a water lily.
Mam's favourite.'

It's not like his other drawings, that have burst from the cracks and brought themselves to life.

This one feels as though it's dying. Like it's slowly being worn *away away away* by the thousand footsteps that are trying to forget that once upon a time a living thing bloomed here.

He puts my camera back in its holder so my view changes to the sky, where – in the distance – I can see the bell tower. Wesley's finish line throwing the world into shadow.

And I want to look away. I want to keep walking. I want to push it to the back of my mind.

I swallow.

'Don't you get annoyed? At people walking over your painting?'

> *I look at the mistake under my trainers.*
> *'Some things are better forgotten.'*
> *Flowers blooming from a Monopoly world.*
> *Her smile as she held him.*
> *O U T.*
> *My insides jump and I cough them back down.*
> *'Listen,*
> *the bank's gonna close.*
> *I should . . .'*

'I've got to go, anyway,' I lie.

He puts his hand up to disconnect the stream and I watch as the colour drains.

Rowan is no longer streaming.

49

Alice

It's taken half an hour and several spoons to muster the courage to type his name into Google.

Wesley Cooper.

Every letter dredges up a new memory from that day. The way the sun bled into the clouds. The starburst glare from the red traffic light. The shadow in the window of the car driver's seat before the stream went dead.

Just like Rowan's floor painting. I've buried it underfoot in the hope that eventually it all gets worn away. But what if I stopped staining the soles of my feet? What if I tilted my perspective? What if I stopped and looked and saw the life that once bloomed on the other side of the camera?

The truth is, I didn't know Wesley at all. It took some digging in Screen Cast for me to even find out his surname. I know that he wore his watch on his right hand. I know that he rode his bike to work and at weekends. I know that he used to love to go as fast as he possibly could.

But I don't know anything of the man who got all those hundreds of people to turn up at his funeral. Or of the person who passed a note to my mum to say that he saw something special in Rowan. Something that I see, too.

I press enter.

I expect him to come up as the top result, but instead I see pages from businesses and people living whole worlds away. I'm about to give up when I click search videos.

And there, at the top, is a picture of the handlebars of a bike. Wesley's bike.

My throat clogs. Something inside me is telling me to close the window, shut my eyes and pretend that I never searched for his name. But I don't. I force my mouse to hover over the video.

And I click play.

50

WesleyCycles67

And now I am back with Wesley, speeding along streets lined with people. And he's cycling so fast that their faces blur into lines and their cheers stretch out like passing sirens.

My heart is beating a million times a minute, because he's going too fast. He's going too fast.

But he's also not going fast enough.

Ahead of him is another cyclist, head down but body standing in its seat, forcing legs to pump so hard that the bike swings from left to right. On the rider's back is the number twenty-four and ahead is a finish line wrapped in gold and this person's going to get there first.

I can hear Wesley's breaths bursting behind me like a steam train. As if nothing – not even a speeding car – could ever stop them.

The camera shakes and swings. The hands gripping the handlebars flush red.

He's gaining on number twenty-four. So fast that soon the cyclist's head next to him swings round to face us – their expression a flash of surprise before we're gone again. And it reminds me of the joy we felt, passing the traffic-stuck cars on our final day together. The looks on the faces of the drivers as they realized that one man on a bicycle could beat a two-tonne car.

Wesley leans back and his hands disappear from his handlebars as the finish-line tape bursts against the camera. And I can hear him. Panting and laughing. His fists flying into view, clenched and impossibly strong.

'I did it,' a voice says from behind me. 'Yes!'

The bike slows to a stop in the crowd where people of all ages are jumping up and down and cheering. And the camera is lost for a moment within their smiles and screams, before hands pick me up and spin me round.

And there – floating in a sea of people – is a man.

A yellow-striped helmet is strapped to his head, and purple sunglasses reflect a camera back at me. He's wearing a fitted top that's so tight, it's like he himself has been painted blue and green. And curling through the gaps in all of this are shocks of bright red hair.

This is Wesley. The Wesley on the other side of the camera.

And although it's the same Wesley I was with when he died, here he's something else, too. A Wesley worth remembering.

A Wesley who Lived.

51

Rowan

And now I am in a bedroom that isn't mine.

A single bedframe is pushed into a corner under a window, the faded striped bedspread still messy with sleep. The walls are a deep royal blue, like we've been swallowed by a whale along with a rickety wardrobe, an old radio and a desk littered with utility bills and final notices.

I'm in Rowan's room. Alone. With him.

> *I should have tidied.*
> *Actually, I should've just told her*
> *I'm busy.*
> *Instead, I just hover at the door,*
> *wondering whether it's weird*
> *to sit on my bed*
> *with a girl who's not really there.*

'So this is your room,' I say.

> *'Yeah, sorry about the mess.*
> *Doing homework with Jonah and*

haven't got round to tidying yet.
What's up?'

I'm still clutching my phone with my message on it asking him if we could chat. He jumped online so fast that I haven't entirely worked out what I'm going to ask him yet. Plus, we're both staring at his bed. And even though I stare at a bed all day every day, his is like a different world. A world of quiet. A world where his body warms with sleep. It's very distracting.

I cough. 'You don't have any art up on the walls?'

I look around.
'I don't really spend much time in here.
Just a place to crash.'
Plus, all my pictures —
every single one —
are in Mam's room.

'Yeah, me neither,' I lie.

I pull on the ends of my hair, scrunching my face up, because I can hear him working out a question to ask me and that's not why I'm here.

'Could-you-take-me-up-the-bell-tower-tomorrow?' I say, fast, so it all comes out as one word.

The air leaves the room.
I sink down the wall.
'Huh?'

'The bell tower,' I say, slower this time. 'I heard your friend Charlie say that there might be a way up? Only I need to remember a – a friend – and it was the last thing he saw, so I thought perhaps –'

'No.'
I say it louder than I planned, but.
'No.
I'm not –
not up there.'

'Oh,' I whisper.

From the floor, things in his room look different. The soft world of the bed is far away. There's dust gathering at the edges of the carpet. Dropped drawing pins point to the ceiling.

'I didn't mean . . . It's just my friend. He – he died, you see. And I was hoping that –'

'I ain't going up there.'
I should be listening,
but my head is filled with
Mam.
Jonah.
That word.
Died died died.

'That's okay,' I say quietly. 'We don't have to.'

I can hear him breathing like he's been running. Or perhaps like I used to when I saw the bell tower beyond my

curtains. But for me that always meant remembering Wesley –
remembering that he'd never reach his finish line.

So what does it mean for Rowan?

'If you want to talk about anything, you know . . .'

> *I pinch my eyes.*
> *'No. Sorry, I'm being stupid.*
> *It's just –*
> *I'm afraid of heights.*
> *That's all.'*
> *Lying feels like coming up for air.*
> *'Yeah – that's it.'*
> *I give a mock shiver.*
> *'I'll keep on solid ground, thanks.'*

It feels strange that a boy whose favourite place is at the top of
a climbing frame should be afraid of heights, but I laugh.

'Oh! Oh, I see. Yes, probably not, then.'

> *My head is still in my hands,*
> *but she can't see that.*
> *'Yeah. It'd be like you driving, eh?'*

I purse my lips.

'Well, that's the thing, you see. My friend – the one who
died – he was knocked off his bike in a car accident. So it's not
that I'm afraid of cars as such, just that . . .'

> *I stare at the paint under my fingernails.*

'Yeah. I get it.'

'Maybe there's something else we can do instead?'

> *I got up again and*
> *dust myself off.*
> *'Yeah, sure, whatever.*
> *Why don't you text me a list of ideas*
> *and we'll do them tomorrow?*
> *Right now, I've got to . . .'*
> *Check on Jonah.*
> *Make sure he's still*
> *breathing.*

'Yes,' I say. 'Yes, of course.'

I watch his hand hover over the door handle. And something feels awkward. Strange. In a way that it hasn't between us before.

> *'I'm sorry about your friend.'*

From my bed, I look out beyond the flowers on my window sill, to where the bell tower rises.

'Yes. Me too.'

Rowan is no longer streaming.

52

Alice

I wait until Mum is just about to leave for the shops before I ask her, so she won't have as much time to sit down with the answers.

'What was Wesley like to work with?'

She stops checking how much shampoo I have left and her eyebrows disappear into her curls.

'Erm – wow. Wesley. You're talking about him now?'

I keep my eyes on my duvet and she slides herself on to it, shopping bag still over her arm.

'Well, he was nice. Bit of a joker. Cared a lot about the kids. Drank way too much coffee and had the most awful temper on him when he got going. He had this thing about gum and, if he caught anyone in his class with it, you'd hear him ranting two classrooms along.' She smiles. 'But he was lovely really. The school's a darker place since he left.'

I write 'coffee' and 'gum' in my head, next to 'cycling', in my list to send to Rowan. Then Mum takes my hand.

'What was he like as a streamer?'

I plaster a smile on my face before it even registers that's what I'm doing. 'Oh, he was wonderful.'

Mum looks at me for a moment, waiting for more. And I let the moment stretch as an aeroplane goes by outside and Dad calls up, asking if she can put more salmon on the list.

She smiles and gets up. 'Fair enough,' she says.

I wait until she leaves, then dig out my phone and text the list to Rowan.

He replies straight away.

All right, got an idea. Two hours.

Two hours.

I want to delve into Google, looking for more videos of Wesley now I've brought him back to life. But every one of those is a dropped spoon.

Watching videos = 1 spoon

And I'm saving them all for Rowan.

I set an alarm. Close my eyes. And wait to Live again.

53

Rowan

And now I am with someone who's helping a boy with bright yellow hair fix a helmet on to his head.

'Hold still,
will you?'

'I don't want to wear a helmet! Benji doesn't have to wear one,' the boy – Jonah – moans.

Behind us, another boy with spiky hair sniggers behind his hand. And then I notice what he's sitting on.

'Bikes . . .'

Oh shit.
She spoke.
I don't have my earphones in
so I'm pretty sure Jonah heard her.
I freeze.

Jonah stops squirming and looks so hard into the camera, it's like he can see me. And I notice that he has the same dark-cave eyes as Rowan.

'Who's that?' he says.

'Never you –'

'I'm Alice,' I say. 'Pleased to meet you, Jonah.'

Jonah blinks for a moment before putting out his finger and tapping the camera lens, so all I can see is the whorl of a fingerprint.

He's gonna freak out
or ask questions
or say something rude.

Then he smiles. Wide, so I can see he has a tooth missing at the back.

'We're riding bikes. Are you riding with us, too, Alice?'

Bikes. Riding bikes.

I drop my voice.
'Only if you want to.
I understand if not.'

Jonah clips his helmet on, like he's forgotten that he didn't want to wear it. Behind him, his friend peers over, trying to see who they're talking to.

And it's me. It's me – like I'm there. Like I'm sitting astride my own bike, with my feet on the pedals, a yellow-striped helmet on my head and the whole cycle path at my feet.

'Yes,' I say. 'Yes, I'm riding bikes, too.'

Jonah smiles like he's really seeing her.
And it makes me want to
duck down
and look with him.

Jonah scampers off and picks up a rusty-looking bike with stabilizers on. His friend Benji doesn't have them, but neither of them seems worried about that. They push off and I watch them, riding and *talking talking talking* excitedly, out of breath, about nothing and everything, riding all over the pavement and in loops.

'Stay where I can see you!'
I pick up the bike I borrowed from Charlie.
It's a BMX and honestly
I don't know how people ride these.
I think Jonah's old
rust-bucket bike
is bigger than this one.
'You definitely sure?' I say to Alice.

Rowan crouches on his bike and I can see handlebars and the path stretching out before us. I suck in a lungful of breath.

'Yes. Yes, I'm sure. Now go – catch up with them. You're losing them.'

She's right.
The little sods are miles away already.
I push off and my legs groan.

And we're riding. We're riding. And it's nothing at all like riding with Wesley ever was. Rowan thrashes like a fish caught in a net, and the path swings left and right as his legs do, too. And the trees on either side of us blur by, and people walking dogs pull them back to let us past and –

We're free.

We're Living.

I can hear her
laughing.
It makes me feel like laughing, too.
So I cycle faster.

There's a tunnel up ahead and sitting at the mouth are the boys, waiting for us to catch up while also trying to ram their tyres into each other. And I know Rowan sees them, but he doesn't slow down.

We skid round them and their heads snap up.

'See ya later, losers!'
Their shouts echo in the tunnel.
I look back quick

and see they're following.

The tunnel is filled with words, but no sea creatures, and so we spurt out the other end and whip round a bollard in the middle of the path to keep going – going. And I can hear bikes right behind us now and shouts – high-pitched and breathless – and I pedal my own legs like it might help Rowan go faster – faster.

But he's slowing down.

> *Oh*
> *my*
> *God.*
> *This bike.*
> *I think I might*
> *die.*

Jonah and Benji shoot out from behind us like fireworks and roar off ahead and Rowan skids to a halt.

> *'Okay. Okay.*
> *You guys win.*
> *Stop here, okay?*
> *The old people need a rest.'*

'Speak for yourself,' I say, because I feel like I have spoons and spoons left to give. I've been on the back of the wind and raced cars and been round the world – and I've got what it takes to win.

I ditch the bike.
Sit on a bench.
My breath
H E A V E S.
The kids are laughing at me,
but they're listening at least.
They've found some sticks
to sword-fight with.

'Didn't you bring any water?'

'That.
That would have been a good idea.'
I cough and rub my knees.
'Did it help, though?
Remembering your friend?'

I smile. 'It's better than going up a bell tower would have been. Although Wesley was a much better cyclist than you.'

My eyes search for it
haunting the skyline.
'You say your friend was Wesley?
My art teacher who died was called that.'

'Yes, he was your art teacher.'

I stop panting.
'Your friend was my middle-aged art teacher . . .?'

I'm lost in a memory.

'He had a really beautiful bike, you know. Carbon fibre and painted the colour of a galaxy. And when he rode it, he rode it with everything he had. Everything that was Living. When we were on that bike, we were Alive and nothing else mattered.'

'We?'
The penny sort of drops and I can feel it
PINBALLING
down my ribs.
'He streamed for you, too.'

The breeze moves the trees in front of us so the view behind starts building from tiny shards, like one of Rowan's paintings. And, dot by dot, I see a seaside town in a valley of green hills, snapping off into blue.

'Do you think . . .'

I swallow.

'Do you think, that if I hadn't been watching, he would have slowed down? That he would have seen the car?'

Oh,
Alice.
I grip the bench like she might be able
to feel it.

'You were watching.'
And it's not a question, because
from the hollows in her voice
I know she was.

I don't know why it's easier to talk about it with Rowan – a
boy that I've never even met – than it is with Mum. Maybe it's
because he can't see me. Or that, right now, I can't see him,
either.

'The bell tower was the last thing he saw. Before the car
came out of nowhere and – and stopped him seeing altogether.'

I let out my breath slowly.
'I'm sorry I couldn't take you up.
Just –
something happened. Up there.
Jonah's always bugging me to take him, but –'

'It's okay,' I say quietly. 'You don't have to tell me.'

But the thing is,
even this,
the worst thing,
I want her to see and make
beautiful.

He swings round to check on Jonah and Benji, poking at
something in a tree. And then I see his hands squeezing his
legs like he's clinging on to something that's falling away.

I wish. I wish I were there to be solid for him.

'After Dad left,
Mam's drinking got worse.
She'd get into these
dark places
and the only thing that seemed to brighten them
were my paintings.'

I hunt for the places his paintings lurk in the distance – the tunnel by the playground and next to the sea; the castle climbing frame; the pavement in town. But we're too far away to see even a hint of colour.

I lick my lips.
'At some point, they stopped working.
So I tried to go bigger. Better.
Fill the whole world with colour just for her.'
My ribs feel tight.
'I drew the water lilies.
You wouldn't have seen from the alleyway,
because to see them properly
you had to go up.
High.'

His knee is quivering and I wonder if he's cold or just afraid. I grip my laptop, tight.

'I broke into the bell tower with her.

She was already drunk, but
I thought I could snap her out of it somehow.'
I shake my head.
'And I took Jonah.
He was only four.
We climbed up to the top
and I tried to get her to see
– look
– stop.
For just a moment.'

He breaks off and I can almost feel his body like an engine, powering up to explode into something.

'It's okay,' I whisper.

'She – she was swaying all over.
Dancing around, singing about flowers.
I tried to stop her, but –'
The words feel like acid.
'She picked
Jonah
up
and she held him
OUT
over the edge.'

My stomach lurches and I'm pleased that Rowan swings round to check on his little brother again, now laughing hysterically and chasing his friend round the tree.

His breathing splinters.

> 'I just –
> She was smiling.
> Smiling as she held him.
> And his eyes were so –
> confused.'

His voice cracks and I touch my screen like he might be able to feel it.

> I sniff.
> 'Anyway.
> I screamed at her in the same way
> Dad used to, before he left.
> I pulled Jonah away from her and
> I wouldn't let her near him again.
> Not even when we got home.
> And her drinking got worse.
> And eventually
> she disappeared.'

'I'm so sorry,' I say quietly.

> I nod at my shoes.
> 'I just wish I'd been able to
> protect her
> in the way I thought I could.'

'You were just a kid yourself. It's not supposed to be that way round.'

Jonah's laughter spikes through the speakers.

'Do you think he remembers?'

> *I shrug.*
> *'I don't –*
> *I can't talk to him about it.*
> *But he must remember something,*
> *because he's desperate to get up there.*
> *"See the flowers," he says.*
> *But I can't take him.*
> *I've gotta protect him –*
> *especially from that.'*

I sigh, long and low.

'Could you hold your hands together?'

> *I'm too busy staring out into the distance*
> *at the tower that almost*
> *killed everything.*
> *'Huh?'*

'Put your hands together.'

> *I hook one hand*
> *inside the other*
> *like a prayer.*
> *'Why?'*

'Because,' I say softly, 'I very much want to hold your hand right now, but I can't, so you're just going to have to do it yourself.'

And there she goes again.
Shining a light in the darkest of places.
'I failed her,' I whisper.

I squeeze my own hands, tight.

'You did beautiful things, Rowan. None of that is a failure. You know, Wesley was watching you. My mum said. He marked you out as someone special. Someone who could achieve great things.'

I laugh.
'Yeah – Mr Cooper thought
everyone was special.
He put up every crappy painting like it
deserved a prize.'

'Maybe. But, you know, he told my mum that you were different. That you could really be something.'

I swallow.
'Yeah, well, no offence to the dead,
but he didn't know what he was on about.'

I drop my voice to a whisper so it doesn't scare him offline again. Not like last time.

'I see it, too, you know.'

You see the good in everything.'
I stare at the bell tower
knifing into the clouds in the distance.
'I've got other stuff to worry about.
Heating bills and
jobs and
a whole other human to protect.'

'But isn't there something you want for yourself?'

And
of course there is.
Of course.
'Yeah.
There's something.'

'Well, go get it! I don't mean to pry like last time, I really don't, but there are all sorts of ways you can paint, Rowan. You can do courses from home now, in your spare time. Or you can go to college after w—'

'No. Not that.'
Where would I get the money for that?
'I mean —'
And it sort of feels like
JUMPING
when I've got no idea if she's even got a net.

> '*I mean –*
> *I want –*
> *you,*
> *Alice.*'

'I –'

Oh. My chest waterspouts and seems to drag my insides out.

Me. He wants me.

> *Silence ain't golden.*
> '*Listen.*
> *I love streaming for you. I do.*
> *But –*
> *I don't know, Alice –*
> *don't you want more?*
> *Don't you want to be here?*
> *In real life?*'

I do I do I do.

More than anything, I do. But I can't, can I?

That's not my real life.

'I –'

> *Jonah*
> *PLOUGHS*
> *into me.*

All I see is yellow hair.

'Rowan! Rowan! Benji ate some berry sweets from that tree and now he's got tummy ache.'

Oh Christ.
I stand up.
See Benji
CLUTCHING
his stomach.
(Talk about timing, dude.)
'Alice. I'm sorry, I –'

'Go!' I say.
Relief prickles me.

'I need to call his mum . . .'
I don't want to disconnect.
I want to do what Alice said.
Take something for me.
I feel my words hanging like weights from my bones.
But who knows what the hell those berries were.
'I'm sorry.'

Rowan is no longer streaming.

54

Alice

He wants me.

He wants. Me.

In my dream, we're together, suspended in blue. He's floating just a few centimetres above me – so close that I can feel the water rippling between us like an electric current.

His eyes are like dark oceans and they're looking at me. Only me. He's smiling – just enough to reveal a whisper of a dimple in his right cheek. And his hair waves like seaweed above him.

His eyes move slightly and I feel them flutter over my lips, my cheeks, my shoulders. And things are wonderful. Perfect. Almost impossible. Until my hunger flips and I reach out my hand.

He swishes away, using limbs like powerful fins. He's still smiling at me and this time he's asking me to go with him. Up, up, to where the water breaks. His legs kick, and his arms carve the water like butter, until he's torpedoing to the surface.

I kick my legs, too. I battle my arms and wrench my body. But instead of going up with him, I sink. Lower. Lower.

Above me, he breaks the surface with a gasp. I reach out my hand. Try to cry out. And disappear into the black.

55

Alice

I wake up feeling tired, like I really have been swimming.

Dad comes in with breakfast and reads the paper out to me while I eat, stealing bites of sausage.

My phone buzzes. I ignore it.

Dad looks up. 'You not going to get that?'

I shake my head, nodding at the paper. 'Carry on.'

He does, reading something about a new use for horse manure, and my phone goes off again. And again.

He puts the newspaper down. And picks my phone up.

I leap on him. 'Dad!'

He bats me off. 'Rowan, eh? That's your teenage delinquent streamer friend, isn't it? What's he done to get in your bad books?'

I wrench the phone from him and stuff it under my pillow next to the sequin star.

'It's called privacy, Dad.'

I can feel myself blushing and Dad smiles, popping a slice of avocado into his mouth. 'Oh, I see. He's in your *good* books! Well, well, my little Alice is in love.'

I pick up a pillow and stuff it over my face. 'Oh my God.'

He pokes my leg. 'You know, we never had "the talk", did we? The old birds and bees. Well, Alice, when two consenting humans love each other an appropriate amount –'

I bat the pillow at him and tip my breakfast on to the floor in the process. He laughs, ducking out of the way. 'Spoons! Spoons!' he shouts.

'Shut. Up. Then,' I say with each hit.

He holds his hands up and I stop. 'Look what you did to the carpet,' he says, scooping egg up and pausing only a moment before eating it.

I grimace. 'That's it. Room ban. Your privileges have been revoked.' He goes to argue, but I point to the door. 'Out.'

He picks up his paper and shuffles out. And I think that to be the last of it until he turns in the doorway, dropping his face to serious. 'But honestly, Alice. Protection is very important. That anti-virus software on your laptop is getting way out of da–'

I throw the pillow at the door and he disappears.

Fighting with Dad = 3 spoons

I get my breath back, panting as Manta swims round and round his tank in alarm.

'It's okay,' I say to him. 'It's just Dad being silly.'

But my phone burns under my pillow. I take it out and see three messages, all from Rowan.

> Benji is fine – berries not poisonous,
> just not fit for human consumption.

His mum didn't even murder me.

New lease of life.

Want to spend it with me tomorrow?

Yes. Yes. Yes, I do.

But I'm also afraid. Because what if he asks me again to come and see him? To sit on a bench with him and hold his hand. To perhaps lean in as he says again that he wants. Me.

How could I possibly ever say no to that, like I actually have a choice?

My thumbs hover over my phone.

Yes! Take me to class? I want to see
what the mantis and the mudskipper
do next.

It's enough, I think. To show him that I want to be with him. But in a place where he can't ask too many questions. Where he can't ask me to join him.

My heart kicks when a new message comes in from him.

See you there.

56

Rowan

And now I am walking along the metal-cage divide between
the primary and secondary schools, my eyes sliding between
the bars to look for blond hair in the swarm of kids the
other side. They're all screaming like they're in a disaster
movie.

> *I watch her name switch to*
> *green.*
> *'Hi, Alice,' I whisper.*

My insides tumble. 'Hi.'

Walking ahead of him, I see Fran and Charlie, who are
dressed today in matching purple boiler suits and bickering.

'Where are we going?'

> *Just to lunch.*
> *Charlie said he's got to show me something first.*
> *Won't take a minute.*
> *That okay?'*

Fran looks back and Rowan coughs, like he wasn't just talking to himself.

And yes – it's okay. As long as his friends are around, he can't talk to me. Ask me things I can't answer.

We follow the fence round the corner of a classroom, through an open gate into the primary-school side, and towards an old fire door stuffed into crumbling brick.

Rowan freezes.

'No,' I say to Fran,
who spins round, already rolling her eyes.

Rowan's hands are out, fists tight, and I can almost hear his heart jumping out of his chest.

Charlie looks around and takes a long metal crowbar out of his backpack.

'Oh,' I whisper. I've never seen a crowbar before, other than in films. I thought they were just made-up fantasy things – tools to get cartoon characters into treasure chests.

Charlie runs his fingers down the side of the old fire door, like that's his treasure.

'Come on, Ro,' Fran says, her eyes softening. 'We used to do this all the time, remember? Ditch registration – picnic on the top of the world?' She waves a sandwich at him. 'It's been ages since we hung out. We miss you.'

I can't breathe.
Fran looks at the fire door and sees

> *a wormhole to the past.*
> *And I miss it. I do.*
> *I miss using Charlie as a pillow.*
> *I miss arguing with Fran over tags.*
> *I miss being on top of the world and*
> *not caring about a thing in it.*
> *But I don't see that any more.*
> *I see . . .*

Rowan looks up and my view tilts with him, following broken brick as it shoots up into the sky and disappears.

I suck in my breath. 'The bell tower?'

I've never seen it this close up. How the paint is chipped away on the door. How the rust has settled in.

> *Charlie starts hammering at the brick,*
> *chipping bits off until he makes a handhold and*
> *pulls.*
> *The door screams open.*

'Yes!' Fran says, like she can't quite believe it, running forward to help Charlie yank back the door.

Rowan backs off as the bricks around the entrance break off. Fran laughs. 'Charlie, you've ruined this door.'

> *Charlie pulls off the metal handle altogether,*
> *laughing as the door swings wide*
> *like an open jaw.*
> *He looks at me.*

'Souvenir for you, Ro.' Charlie throws the now useless handle to Rowan, but he doesn't try to catch it. It skids noisily across the tarmac.

> *I clear my throat.*
> *'I'm good,' I say.*
> *'Sure you guys want some alone-time, anyway.'*

He turns his back on them and from behind him I hear Fran.

'Don't be like that! Come on, we never hang out any more. It's the bell tower, Rowan!'

But that's exactly it. It's the bell tower – the place that Rowan must see every time he closes his eyes. The place he brought his mum and Jonah.

The place that nearly cost him everything.

> *'You've changed!' Fran calls from behind me.*
> *I ignore her.*
> *Walk back round the buildings to the canteen*
> *where the noise can settle my heartbeat.*

'Are you okay?' I whisper to him.

> *I open the door to the dining hall*
> *and grab a sandwich from the side.*
> *'I'm fine. Sorry about that.*
> *We used to go up there all the time.*
> *They don't know about what happened, so –'*

I take a deep breath.
'Let's just get some lunch, yeah?'

He shows the canteen person a card and is waved through
into the dining hall. And –

Teenagers – more than I've ever seen together in one go –
crowd tables and hang off chairs dotted round the room.
Some eat from old takeaway tubs and some nibble at
sandwiches in packets like Rowan's. Some congregate in
black; others wear oversized, brightly coloured jumpers.

All of them are talking. Laughing. Stealing chips from
each other's plates and sharing videos on their phones.

I head for a free table in the corner
where I can gather my thoughts.

I want to ask him more about what he used to do with
Fran and Charlie. Why doesn't he tell them anything
any more, about what happened at the bell tower? About
Jonah?

But, if we're alone, he might start asking me questions,
too.

'Stop!' I shout, blood humming in my ears. 'Um – wait – I
need you to go and sit with someone.'

I stop walking so fast a girl next to me
chokes on her milkshake.
'Who?' I whisper out of the side of my mouth.

Who who who?

I clutch my pillow and feel the edges of the pink star buried under it.

'Cecelia,' I say. 'Cecelia Adebayo. She's in – my year. The one below you, I suppose.'

> *I spin round on the spot.*
> *'Name doesn't ring a bell.*
> *What she look like?'*

I search the crowd for her face as he turns.

'Dark hair – box braids. She wears glitter nail varnish. She's popular, so she'll be in a crowd – maybe with the climbing club?'

> *'Climbing club?*
> *Don't think we have one of those.*
> *You sure she goes to this school?'*

'Yes, I –'

And then I see her. At the back, in the corner. And my insides soar, because it's her – it's her – but also it doesn't look anything like her.

She's sitting alone. Her head down but her eyes up, chewing a sandwich like she can't eat it fast enough. And she's not smiling or laughing or throwing chips at her many friends.

It's like seeing a whole different person stuffed inside the skin of someone I know like I know myself.

'There,' I say. 'In the corner, with the purple braids.'

> *I walk over.*
> *'You sure you know this girl?*
> *I'm not just gonna sit down and look*
> *weird, am I?'*

'No, you can't tell her that I'm here. In fact, hide the camera. Cover me up.'

> *I sigh,*
> *balancing my sandwich on my knee*
> *as I zip my hoodie up over her.*
> *'You won't be able to see now, though.'*

I'm lost in grey. 'I can still hear. Go! Sit next to her.'

> *I don't know*
> *W H Y*
> *I'm doing this.*
> *I pull up a chair*
> *and purple braids eyes me like a*
> *frightened hare.*
> *'Um – can I sit here?'*

I don't catch her reply, but she must say yes, because I hear him fumble with the chair and put his sandwich on the table.

'What's happening?' I whisper.

I roll my eyes.
There's no way I'm talking to myself
next to some girl
no one seems to know.

There's just silence. I hear him rip open his sandwich packet. The click of a water bottle opening.

But no Cecelia. Nothing to tell that she's even there at all.

'Ask her something! Ask her if she had climbing practice today.'

That'll make me seem less like a stalker.
I clear my throat.
'So – um – I heard that there's a climbing club?'
Purple braids' head shoots up.
She looks behind her,
like she's expecting a prank.

'Yeah. So?'

It's her. Her voice. And she's speaking to Rowan. Looking at him eating his lunch.

And I've never wanted to be at any table more.

'Nothing – just that's cool.'
She still looks frightened and, to be honest,
I don't blame her.
I sigh.
'So you know Alice?'

My blood turns to concrete. 'Don't mention me!' I hiss.

> *Purple braids glares at me like*
> *poison.*

'Look, whoever put you up to this, it's not funny, okay? I'm eating my sandwich, so just piss off and leave me alone.'

> *I put my hands up.*
> *'No one put me up to this.'*
> *I hear Alice suck in a breath.*
> *'Okay – well, Alice did.*
> *But she doesn't want me to mention her*
> *for some reason.'*

He says the last bit loudly, to make sure I can hear him.

I can. I can hear all of it like it's happening inside my own head. Like a nightmare.

'Alice did – what? She doesn't . . .' Cecelia trails off.

> *Her eyes travel down to the*
> *lump under my hoodie.*
> *And she shakes her head.*

'Seriously, Alice?'

My name. She said my name.

And I'm not sure if I want Rowan to unzip his hoodie and let me out, or pick up his tray and run away. But then I hear the scrape of a chair.

Purple braids leans over,
pointing a finger in my face.
I shrink.

'You – whoever you are. You show her one testicle and I swear
I will hunt you down and chop it off. Don't think I won't.'

Holy shit.

I'm sawn in half.

Part of me jumps – soars – dances at her showing that she
secretly still cares about me in her own messed-up and entirely
petrifying way. And the part of me with Rowan cringes.

'Um . . .' I croak.
She picks up her sandwich and stomps off,
glaring at me like I'm a pervert.
I unzip my hoodie.
'Yeah . . . you know, maybe it's best
if I come up with the stuff we're gonna do
next time.'

I bite my lip.

'I'm sorry. I'm so – she's really lovely. She's just –'

'A tad overprotective?
Yeah. Got that.'
I take a deep breath.
'I hope you got

*whatever you needed
from that at least.'*

And I can't help it. I smile. Because Cecelia still cares about me. Enough to threaten a perfectly lovely boy.

And that feels like hope.

57

Alice

I'm listening to an old Spice Girls' song. One of Mum's favourites from back in the day.

She left it on accidentally to cover the noise of the washing machine downstairs, but I have enough spoons to listen to it today.

Listening to music = 1 spoon

The song undulates, reminding me of Wesley and our cycle rides. But this time, when I remember them, no car comes out of nowhere and stops us. We just keep riding, down cycle paths overgrown with trees, over railway bridges and the very tops of hills.

And it makes me think of Rowan, too. Cycling next to me because he wants to be. With me.

I just wish I could say that back.

I close my eyes and listen to the peaks and troughs, and long lanes of notes. And it's only when I notice a strange prickle on the tops of my hands that I realize that someone's watching me.

'Cecelia!'

I lean over and smack the music off, struggling up to sitting and trying to brush my hair out of my eyes.

She has her school uniform on and her hand is gripping my bed frame like she might float away. She looks at me. I look at her. And we both start speaking at once.

'You really mustn't pay attention to –'

'You must think I'm a complete –'

We break off. She looks back at the door and then closes it and I try to wipe my sweaty hands down my duvet without her noticing.

It's weird to see her standing at the end of my bed. Usually she's jumping over it, crawling between the sheets with me. She opens her mouth and closes it a few times and, standing next to Manta, she almost looks like a fish, too.

Finally, she says, 'I didn't know, you know. About your illness.'

I find myself laughing her words away, but I stop myself. I stop myself lying. It's time for her to see.

'Yes, you did.'

Her eyes open wide and she comes a step closer to me. 'No, honestly I didn't, Al. You always seemed fine when I came up and always going on about tae kwon do. Like, okay, yes, I knew you weren't very well or whatever, but I didn't know . . . I didn't know it was this bad.'

'It's not bad,' I say quickly. 'I am happy.'

'I didn't mean you couldn't be *happy*, I mean that . . .' She sighs and looks at me. Properly. 'I mean that I'm sorry. I mean that I should have pulled my head out of my own arse for just one minute and actually paid attention. I would never have asked . . .'

I pick at my nails. 'I don't mind you asking. It's nice to be invited to things. It's just that . . . it's just that I can't . . .'

She sits down on the bed. 'I know.'

I shake my head. 'I need to say it.' I take a deep breath. 'I'm sorry I couldn't come to your birthday party, Cecelia. I just . . . I just didn't have the spoons.'

She laughs and I notice that she's crying. 'It was only a party. It was weeks ago, anyway.'

I hold her hands. Tight. 'I should have said it back then. I hid it from you.'

She climbs into bed with me and I smell green tea and climbing walls and Living and I want to hold on to it, tight.

'You're such a mongoose. You don't have to hide shit from me, you know. You could have just said. I'd have understood.'

I shake my head. 'Like you hid, sitting alone at lunch?'

She freezes. 'Yeah, well. Maybe I've been lying about stuff, too. The others at school are dicks, Al. Seriously. Not one of those losers turned up to my birthday party, you know?' She lifts up her head. 'Sometimes I just feel so invisible, it's easier to pretend –'

I nod. 'Pretend that things are different? So I wouldn't leave you, too.' Now I'm crying. 'But I did!'

'Oh Christ.' She rubs the tears from my eyes so her nails dig into my eyebrows. 'I ran away from you, not the other way round. And I only ran because I felt like shit. Real mature, I know, but seeing you that ill . . . I guess I realized what an absolute tool I was for not realizing that my BFF is ILL.

Not, like, a bit down. And not, like, just needs a push to get back out there. But, like, ILL.' She stops rubbing my face. 'I don't even know what you're ill with!'

I laugh. 'Well, that makes two of us.'

She swears again and pulls the duvet up and over us so we're surrounded by darkness. And I can hear her breath and my breath and they're together and the same.

'Okay. So how about this, then? How about you tell me, right now, the stuff you do know, yeah? And how about you tell me what I can do – as your friend and all-round favourite person – to help?'

And so I tell her.

I explain about the spoons and what it means when I drop them.

I explain about the doctor's appointments and the new drugs I'm on.

I explain about why I can't eat Pop-Tarts, or go downstairs on my own, or go to birthday parties. And I explain how I could perhaps listen to a whole CD one day and not stand the sound of my own voice the next. And how it's almost impossible to describe, because it doesn't stick to one set of rules.

'Will you get better?' she whispers.

And my heart. Thumps. 'I don't know,' I say.

And it's the truth. Finally.

Cecelia holds me, tight. 'So what can I do?' she says. 'Tell me and I'll do it. I have a spare kidney, probably, although I did drink a LOT of beer on my birthday, hence the awkward screaming match with you.'

I laugh and I hold her back. 'You can do this.'

'Suffocate you with your duvet?'

'No!' I laugh and hold her hands. 'You. Me. This. And tell me the truth – if things are bad at school. I'm here, too, you know.'

She doesn't make a joke this time. She sees Me. And she's here. And that. That is everything.

She sniffs. 'Don't think I've forgotten about that boy you sent to stalk me at lunch, by the way.'

I pull her into my chest and try not to smile too hard. 'Shhh,' I say. 'You're ruining the moment.'

58

Alice

I get a text later from Rowan.

Meet me tomorrow? x

I look at the kiss at the end of his message. It's only a little letter and Cecelia puts lines of them at the end of her texts, but this one feels different. Like it's leaped from my phone screen and stamped itself into my chest.

Obsessing over a kiss in a text message = 1 spoon

I keep typing my reply and then deleting it again. 'Meet' could just mean hop on to Stream Cast again, like I met him outside the Aquatic Centre. But it could also mean get dressed. Go downstairs. Walk and hold a conversation somewhere where the world roars.

I want to meet him. I want to see what he looks like when he says that he wants me. But that means telling him who that 'me' really is.

Someone who can't go downstairs. Or walk somewhere. Or hold a conversation in a busy place. Would he still want me then?

After dinner, I'm watching a film with Mum when the light from the screen starts to halo. I ignore it and I ignore it, but then the pain starts. Right above my eye. I sigh loudly.

'What's wrong?'

'Nothing.' I stuff my fingers into the pain and rub it hard enough that it might get the message.

'Alice, that won't help a migraine.'

'I've kept well within my spoons today. I've not even left the bed. I don't get this stupid . . .'

Mum turns off the film and starts to squeeze my wrists. I should let her. I should tell her that I'm fine and smile through the pain. But it's just another thing taken away from me and it makes me want to screw the world into a tiny ball and stomp on it. Hard.

I shake her off and turn away.

'I'm sorry, sweetheart.'

She lifts herself off the bed and brings the Me-deadening pill over. Taking those feels like giving up, so I shake my head. She puts it on the bedside table with a glass of water, turns off the light, and leaves.

I should call her back and tell her that I'm sorry and that I'm fine. But the pain gets worse.

I stare at the pill. Stare at my phone. And I hang on for as long as I can until the edges of me start to disintegrate. Then I pick up both.

I wince into my phone screen as I text.

> **Busy tomorrow! Speak soon,**
> **though x**

I turn the phone all the way off. Then I swallow the pill with the water so I can do the same to me, too.

But I hope he sees the kiss I gave him back. And I hope it's enough to make him see that – despite the impossible world between us – I want him, too.

59

Alice

I'm not really here. But Cecelia is.

I watch as she opens her birthday present. Points to her favourite photos in the book I made her. Kisses me on the head.

When dinner arrives, she stays.

She scoops creamed kale on to a spoon. Makes quiet aeroplane noises. Into my mouth.

I try to give her a smile. She sees. It eggs her on.

She makes the spoon duck.

Dive.

Loop-the-loop.

Gets kale all over me. And her. And my duvet.

And, inside, the part of me that remains is laughing.

So hard, I can't breathe.

60

Alice

I'm back to eight spoons. Which isn't enough for me to spend all day on Screen Cast, but enough for me to check my phone for another text from Rowan.

Again. And again. And – because she came round as soon as school was over – Cecelia notices.

She swipes my phone off me and ducks away so I can't reach to snatch it back.

'Cecelia, that's mine.'

'Well, obviously.'

She unlocks it. I really must change the passcode.

'There's nothing on here,' she says, disappointed. 'You know, if you want to keep looking at my face, you can just look at the actual me. I am right here and way better-looking than this stupid photo you have on your lock screen.'

I snatch the phone back. 'I like that photo.'

She's right, though. No messages from Rowan. Not even ones without kisses.

Cecelia is staring. 'You're waiting for a text, aren't you?'

'No,' I say, a little too quickly, putting my phone far away from her.

'Oh my God, you *are*! You're texting someone and you didn't even tell me!' She pokes me in the ribs. 'All the boring doctor shit you talk about, and you withhold actual exciting information from me?' I glare at her and she smiles. 'Who is it, then? Oh! Is it that boy you sent to spy on me at lunch? Because, even though I was threatening him and everything, I was doing so while thinking he was hot.'

I sigh. She's looking at me in the same way as those puppies Dad borrowed.

'Okay,' I say. 'Okay, but if I tell you, you need to promise not to freak out on me and make it weird, okay?'

She mimes a halo around her head. 'Would I ever?'

'Yes.'

She grins.

I close my eyes. Take a deep breath. Try not to drop too many spoons by telling her.

'His name is Rowan.'

She bounds up on to her knees, almost bouncing me off the bed and thumping me on top of my head.

'I knew it, I knew it! The hot one!'

'Cecelia!' I shout.

Wrestling away from Cecelia = 1 spoon

She stops and sinks down to grab my shoulders.

'How? I mean – *how*? I thought you didn't talk to your streamers in case they send you testicle pics?'

'That's not the reason,' I tut. 'He's someone Mum is working with. He's using his phone and we got talking . . .'

She shrieks again. 'Have you met him?'

I shake my head.

'But you want to?'

I look around at my bed and the flannel on the radiator I used to wash myself earlier. 'I can't, though, can I?'

She shrugs. 'Why not? I mean – okay – so you might not be able to walk to the park and meet him or whatever. But surely he can come round here?'

'Oh no, no, no . . . he can't see . . .' The pills on the bedside table. The peeling wallpaper. The walls I live in.

Cecelia squints at me. 'He does know, though, doesn't he? You did tell him you can't, like, see him outside?'

I bite my lip and she bangs her head into the pillow.

'Oh. My. God. Al! What is it with you and keeping this a secret?!'

I sit myself up. 'You don't understand. He thinks I'm just like him and it's . . . it's . . .'

'Fake, is what it is.'

I go to argue. But in the end I just sink back down inside the covers again. Because she's right. It is fake. He wants me, but he has no idea who I really am.

I pull the duvet over my head and she ducks down into it, so we're back inside our own world again.

'Look. You're not like him. You're not like me. You're not like anyone. And you need to stop seeing that as a bad thing.' She shakes me. 'You – are – Alice! And Alice is pretty cool, you know. She's kinda funny. Cute AF. And she's – you know – got Pop-Tarts.'

I wince and she smiles. 'Look, pal, I'm just saying. You clearly like this guy, seeing as you must have checked your phone a bazillion times today. So why don't you give him the chance to like you, too? You know – the actual you?'

My heart is beating too fast and I throw off the covers to get some air.

'I don't know . . .'

But she leans over me. Grabs my phone off the table. And I watch with wide eyes as she clicks on his name, reads back the last few messages and types back a reply for me.

> Hey! Sorry about being AWOL. I'm around Wednesday, if you are? I need to tell you something xxxxxxxxxx

I snatch my phone back to stop the kisses, but it's too late. She's pressed send.

Having a Rowan-based breakdown = 2 spoons

But then my phone buzzes and Cecelia throws her arms up in celebration before she even knows what it says.

> Wednesday. Looking forward xx

61

Alice

It's Sunday and I've been feeling a bit lonely.

I don't usually, but today Mum and Dad have seemed distracted. And I've heard noises from outside my door. Swearing. Whispering. Drilling. So when Dad pops up suddenly by my bed, it surprises me.

'Spoon count.'

My heart leaps and I check my phone, but it isn't Wednesday. I didn't miss it. I didn't miss Rowan.

'Have we moved Wednesday-night Cure Board officially now?'

And then suddenly Cecelia pops up, too. I jump.

'But you're busy Wednesday, aren't you?'

I pretend to be getting over the shock of seeing her while trying to give her the eye without Dad seeing.

He waves his hand. 'Oh, no need to hide it, kiddo. I know all about your secret date with that delinquent.'

I think all the blood has leaked out of me and I shoot daggers at Cecelia. Who is laughing.

Laughing.

'He's not a delinquent,' I say. 'And it's *not* a date. Since when do you listen to anything Cecelia says, anyway?'

Dad elbows Cecelia. 'Since she came up with ammo good enough to make your face do that.' He turns to her. 'You're right, that was fun.'

Mum pops her head round the door. 'What was?'

'Nothing,' we all say together.

She frowns. 'Did you get a spoon count yet?'

'I'm working on it!' Dad turns back to me. 'Go on, then. What we at?'

I've been trying to rest all day. But it's difficult when Cecelia is putting silly ideas in my head and telling Dad about things she most certainly shouldn't be telling him.

'Five or six, maybe?' I say.

Dad and Cecelia look at Mum, who looks out of the door at something else. Then she turns back and nods.

'Master has spoken,' Dad says, and he scoops me up without even asking me, so one of my socks falls off and I barely have time to make sure all the buttons on my top are fully in place.

'Dad!' I shout, clinging on to him.

But Cecelia is racing through the door and my heart is racing through spoons, because he's taking me outside my bedroom again. Out of the four walls and on to the landing.

'Are we going downstairs?' I whisper hopefully.

'Even better.'

He takes me into the spare room.

I can't say that this is usually better than outside, where there are bats and wind and sunsets and Living, breathing things. But the spare room has had a makeover since I was last there and it makes me want to leap down and run across to Mum and Cecelia, sitting on the floor where the washing usually dries, because –

The whole room is green.

A thick piece of bright green material hangs from new hooks in the ceiling, rolling like a grassy hill round the walls either side of it and across the floor to the window opposite, where Dad's set up his laptop and a webcam. And in the middle are props. Feather boas, snorkel sets, an astronaut's helmet and a whole pile of other things my eyes can't pick out.

'What on earth . . .' I say as Dad lays me down next to Mum and Cecelia.

'Wait and see,' Mum says, strapping a snorkel and a mask to my face, so it pinches my nose.

'Ouch! You're not going to flood the room with water, are you? That sounds expensive.'

Cecelia rolls her eyes as she struggles to put on a wetsuit over her clothes. 'Jesus, Al – impatient much?'

Dad fiddles around with his laptop until suddenly a screen propped up against the radiator flickers to life. For a moment, I see me, lying on a bright green carpet next to swearing Cecelia and Mum, who is trying to squeeze into a green Morphsuit.

A thousand questions are sitting on my lips, but they all disappear as Dad presses a button and the screen changes.

And suddenly we're not sitting in the middle of the spare room on the screen. We're floating in the middle of a vast, endless sea.

'Oh – wait – what?' I whisper, trying to crawl over to the screen to see it better.

But there we are. Moving in real time. But, instead of the carpet, on the screen I'm paddling through water. Among silver fish that flick their tails and sharks that circle above us. And I put out my hand to one and my fingers pass right through it.

'Green screen,' Dad says, watching me. 'You can be anywhere you want in this room, kiddo.'

I look around. At Cecelia fist-bumping herself for finally getting into her wetsuit. And at Mum, who has disappeared from the screen completely now she's covered in green. And I can't think of a better place in all the world to be.

First – we swim. Mum holds me up as I pretend to paddle and, on the screen, it really does look like I'm floating. Cecelia pushes herself across the carpet in a backstroke and attempts to punch a shark until I shout at her.

And then – we're floating through space. Cecelia makes throaty Darth Vader noises and Dad calls out from behind the camera all the things that are inaccurate about her impression. Mum helps me roll, spin, float above the world, where the stars twinkle and an asteroid bursts across a black sky.

Then – we're at a party. In front of a heaving mass of bodies, moving in time to music we can't hear. Cecelia dresses us in plastic crowns and feather boas and complains loudly about there being no music until Mum rolls her eyes and starts singing one of her old songs.

Cecelia grabs my wrists and makes my arms dance for me – even though I know all the moves enough to know she's doing them wrong. And I laugh – laugh so hard that I can't see anything but a blur of green and plastic ribbons and Mum's wide smile.

'This is amazing,' I say as Cecelia lets me go.

Dad grins. 'Oh, you ain't seen nothing yet.'

He fiddles around in a box for a moment and then brings something out that looks like a blackened scuba mask.

'Right. Cecelia – you break this and I'm going to make you pay for it in Pop-Tarts for the rest of your life, okay?'

He straps it on my head and the world disappears in darkness.

'What do you mean, me? I'm not even the one wearing it – Alice is!'

'Yes, but Alice is sensible,' Mum says, clicking what feels like headphones over my ears.

'I'm not always sensible,' I say, thinking of Rowan and me breaking into tunnels and skipping school.

Cecelia scoffs and I kick her.

'Okay?' Dad says in my ear.

'I think so . . . But I'm not sure –'

'Patience!' Cecelia shouts.

I wait. Lying on the floor with a black mask on that pinches my forehead and nose. And around me I can hear whispering. I think about the webcam they've got set up and wonder what awful things they're doing to me when the mask flickers to life.

'Oh!' I say as light surrounds me. I blink. And then I see a world blooming to life.

All around me – up, down, left and right – are flowers.

They dance in a breeze I can't feel. And open against a sun that doesn't seem to be reaching me. And stretch as far into the distance as I can see.

I look down and my body isn't there any more. I've left it. I exist only as a pair of eyes and, as I move my head around, more of the world comes into view. And, in my ears, I hear birds. The slow buzzing of bees. The wind through the trees in the distance.

I stretch my hand out until I feel Mum's. I can't see her, but I can feel her. She's there.

'What's it like?' Cecelia whispers from nowhere.

I spin round. 'It's like . . . it's like I'm really here.'

'Borrowed it off a mate at work.' Dad's voice appears from the clouds. 'Virtual reality. If you like it, maybe we can get you one for your birthday next year.'

Mum laughs. 'Not with the amount you spend on salmon.'

I hear a click and the world changes, so now I'm sitting in what seems to be a mining cart at the top of a mountain. And in this world the sky bleeds red and volcanoes erupt all around me.

I laugh. 'Not quite as realistic, this one.'

'Let's see about that . . .' Dad says.

And suddenly the mining cart lurches. I reach out and grab Cecelia's shoulder with my other hand as I speed down tracks on the mountain, lurching left and right and ducking as flying dinosaurs dive for my head. I scream. The cart swings up higher and higher, and ahead of me the track ends altogether, and I put out my feet to stop it, but feel nothing as I'm not really there, and slowly I fall out of the clouds.

I let go of Mum and Cecelia and take off the mask, blinking in the real life around me. Where I'm not falling, but lying in the spare room with a family who are laughing at me.

'Someone else's turn, I think,' I say, feeling slightly sick.

Cecelia grabs the headset off me as Dad warns her about Pop-Tarts again.

I enjoy watching her, exploring spacecraft with robots on the screen, like she really has left this world.

Mum has a go and Dad gives her a set of controllers to hold, so she can swipe at neon bricks with lightsabres. And – because she's still wearing the Morphsuit – on the screen we just see her head floating in a tunnel of light.

Dad has a go and Cecelia pulls me off to the side, laying my head in her lap.

'Maybe you could bring Hot Boy here? Have a virtual date with him in a jungle or something. That would be cool.'

I laugh, staring at the light bulb swinging after Dad just accidentally punched it.

'You know, I think perhaps it's the real things that are the most fun. Like this,' I say, smiling at Mum, who is poking Dad in the ribs and making him jump.

Cecelia mock-faints. 'It's only taken you sixteen years, Alice, but I think you might have actually finally got it.'

62

Alice

Last night, I dreamed I was back in that endless sea.

It was so deep that, when I looked at what I thought was the bottom, I saw only a starburst sun, shining up at me.

Somewhere I could hear the clicks and slaps of life carrying on above the surface. But no matter how long or urgently I swam, I couldn't reach it.

I wake up, gasping.

Mum is there already and has taken the day off, like she knew what was going to happen. I try to tell her about my dream and how yesterday was perhaps the most wonderful day anyone has ever spent, but she shushes me.

'Rest today, love.'

So I do. I eat and I drink, but that's all. And I try to gather up the spoons that I dropped while spinning in space. Occasionally, though, I clench my fists. Try them out: they're working. There isn't any migraine pain, or stomach pain, or mystery bone pain.

My thoughts are whirring and I can remember my name, and Cecelia's name, and Rowan's, too.

And my belly even somersaults when I remember that I'm going to be with him outside soon. Not in real life, because, even without the usual dropped-spoon symptoms, I know the Illness is there somewhere – waiting.

I run through all the different ways I could tell him and all the different ways he could react. Everything from him turning off the phone immediately and never speaking to me again, to the far scarier version of him running straight to my house, into my room, and –

I shake my head.

Mum busies round me, muttering about how stupid it was to force me into the spare room on six spoons. And I want to tell her that actually I think this time I've got away with it.

But also I don't want to jinx it.

I want to just float in this hope a little longer.

63

Alice

It's Wednesday and I'm nervous.

Cecelia keeps messaging lewd things to me and Dad even leaves a note on my pillow telling me not to do anything he wouldn't do, and it's difficult to pretend that today is normal.

I practise what I might say again and again in my head, and it never goes quite right. The Illness is a difficult one to explain to someone – even to Cecelia, who's been seeing it right in front of her for years and years.

She's right, though. It's time for Rowan to see me for who I really am. And if he's really going to see Me, then I'm going to need to use something a little bit different to Stream Cast. I'm going to have to turn my own camera on.

Cecelia races out of school at lunch to help me get ready. She's packed what looks like the contents of her entire bedroom into one beach bag and, before she's even all the way in the room, she's throwing out brightly coloured cardigans and what look like torture devices.

Mum follows at her heels. 'Cecelia? What the hell is –'

'Sorry, Sophia, I love you, but –' She closes the door on Mum's rather shocked-looking face.

I scowl at her and she throws her hands up.

'We. Don't. Have. Time! I only get forty minutes for lunch and have you seen you lately? Dude.'

She jumps on to my bed and hands me a mirror and I make a point of not looking at it.

'I just need to look presentable, okay? I don't need a makeover. I don't need whatever you're planning on doing with those.'

She stops unwinding the hair curlers and sighs. 'Mate – and I say this with all the affection in the world – but you are absolutely clueless.'

I go to argue, but she's suddenly on me with a brush. 'Shut up now. The master is working.'

So I close my eyes and I let her work.

She mutters what I think may well be insults about my 'stupid pale face not matching her tones' and how she 'really has her work cut out', until I sneak an eye open and she stops talking.

She must be able to find something, though, because she rubs a sherbet-smelling cream into my skin, and dusts me for fingerprints. She pokes at my eyeballs with a brush and makes me blink on to another.

And then she kisses me. Right on the lips. I look at her, surprised, and she smiles.

'That, Alice, is how hot you look.' She sits back and holds up a mirror.

I'm expecting to see someone completely different. Or perhaps just myself looking a mess. But I don't look like that. I just look like me. Only a bit more even.

I assume that's it, but she makes me sit still while she drowns me in dry shampoo and burns me with hair curlers.

'I'm done, I'm done! Now go, clear off.'

She grins and kisses my forehead this time. 'Knock him dead. Not literally. It is on camera after all.'

I smile at her as she almost cartwheels out.

'Cecelia!' I call as she leaves. 'Thank you.'

She blows me a kiss, and closes the door.

I check my watch. I have an hour and a half before I'm due to speak to Rowan – between his afternoon work shift and picking Jonah up from school. It's enough time to take off the awful clothes Cecelia made me wear and squeeze myself into my black birthday dress. And try to let my mind empty completely, before it gets packed full of worries again.

At two forty, I take a moment to breathe. Check my spoons. Take out my laptop.

I open the same video-call app that we used to call Dr Rahman. But instead of choosing her name, I copy Rowan's number instead.

And I turn my camera. On.

My insides leap seeing my own face in the corner. Looking strange, but not in a bad way. I steady the laptop on a pile of pillows so behind me he'll be able to see the window. The flowers Mum brought me that are bent in prayer.

And me. Here. Alive.

I grip my laptop, tight. And click.

Calling **Rowan** . . .

64

Rowan

And now I am standing at the edge of the sea as the sun hole-punches through a hazy film of cloud. The water tosses and churns, raking in stones from the beach and coughing them back out again.

My insides somersault, both with how beautiful it looks and with the disappointment of not seeing Rowan's face. He must still have his phone in the harness round his chest.

'Hi,' I say nervously.

Alice.
Her voice whispers through my earphones.
'Hey.
So – how was your busy time?'
Was she even doing anything?
Or was she just
avoiding me?

'It was . . . eventful,' I say.

On my lips are the same sort of lies I used to tell Cecelia. Where I'd blur the edges of virtual living and real life, to make it seem as though I was off doing impossible things. But that's just the thing, isn't it?

Diving under seas. Floating through space. Going to a party. They're not real.

I scrunch my eyes. Squeeze my fists.

'Could you – could you turn the camera round? To face you.'

I almost want to say
NO.
That it's not fair that I keep
giving her so much of me
when I have no idea if she's even alive.
But also – it's Alice.
And a bigger part of me wants to keep
giving her everything.
I pick up the phone
and turn it.

And now I am standing on a beach, facing a boy.

His face is almost dyed gold from the sun behind me. His hair is tied messily back from his face, but a few strands have escaped. One is sticking to his lips and, as I look at him, he sweeps it back.

And he's looking. At me.

For a moment, I don't even register.
But then
– there's a girl on my screen.
Ghost-white.

Wide eyes that see everything.
And so
bone-achingly beautiful
that the sea seems to freeze mid-wave.
'Alice?'

He sees me. He sees me. He sees Me.

I'm not just the watcher. And if a car comes roaring through my bedroom wall, he will see it smash through my body. I am here. I am Alive.

And I think I might be hyperventilating.

'Hi,' I squeak.

She's rocking out these big
deep
breaths.
Looking around her
at walls and a window.
'Hey, hey.'
I sit down like that might help somehow.
'What's wrong?'

'Nothing!' I say and I try to smile. I tuck my hair behind my ears and I keep looking at myself in the corner. 'I suppose I'm just not used to being the one on camera.'

She's nervous.
And I wonder if I should tell her that

she doesn't have anything to be nervous about.
That it's me. Rowan.
And, for me, seeing her face feels like
flying.
I clear my throat.
'Would it help if I don't look at you for a bit?'
I spin the camera round
so we're back to seeing the same thing
from different worlds.

'Oh –'

The picture changes and on my screen is the sea churning into the exact colour of the sky, so there's no break between the two. It just rolls up, over us, like we're caught in an endless wave that tunnels us – hides us away – propels us to something unknown and deep and beautiful.

But it isn't Rowan.

'That's okay. You can turn me round.'

I spin her back.
'Hi,' I laugh. 'Um –
so you're here!
And that's your face.'
I dither to a halt, kicking myself.

I laugh nervously.

'Am I not what you were expecting?'

His eyes widen.

'No! You're – better.
I mean.'
Jesus Christ.
'To be honest, I didn't imagine you
to look like anything.
You were just this voice-person, you know?'

I bite my lip and then I remember that he can see me now and quickly stop.

'A body-less voice-person sounds quite good.'

Imagine the places I could go without a body to hold me back.

'No, your body is nice –
I mean –
good.'
I sigh into my palm.
'Can you just pretend I'm not talking?'

I laugh for real this time. Seeing him nervous and stumbling makes me feel less nervous somehow. And, with his eyes covered, I can let myself look properly at the perfectly parallel lines of his eyebrows, mouth and jaw. The hint of dark stubble at the end of his chin. The curls of hair that have come loose from their tie and are fluttering in the sea breeze.

'I've been thinking about what you said before,' I whisper. 'About taking something for yourself.'

My heart

LURCHES.
I look at her from between my fingers.

I lick my lips. 'I know you said that art school wasn't an option, but I've been looking, and –'

'Alice . . .'
She stops and I do, too.
I want to remind her that I chose
HER.
But I'm tired of jumping off cliffs
with no safety net.
I sigh.
'I've been looking, too.'

My heart flutters. 'You have?'

'Yeah, you wore me down.
Sort of feels like asking me to
go to the moon.
But I guess some people have been.
Some people make it.'

'It's not impossible,' I smile.

Just sort of unlikely.
'There's a scholarship your pal Wesley
was always on about.
Maybe after A Levels I can

take a look.'
I've managed to hold everything together so far.
Maybe I got this, too . . .

'Well, I think you'd be wonderful.'

When she says it,
she nods
like she's agreeing with herself.
Her fringe bounces into her eyes
(sea blue).
Her lips. Part.
'Alice?
Where are you?'

I stop. Like I've been running so fast that I've stumbled over the edge of the world.

I can feel the wind under me like I might be able to jump on its back and fly. But below there's plummeting and, below that, there are rocks, and even further below that there is absolute nothing, and that scares me the most.

But perhaps this is Living. Perhaps Living isn't staying on the cliff edge and wondering whether you might fly or fall. Perhaps – sometimes – Living is jumping.

'Rowan. I need to tell you something.'

She looks afraid.
But I don't want to turn her round this time.
'So tell me.'

I close my eyes. Take a breath. And really the truth is just like gravity, isn't it?

It's as simple as falling.

'I'm not . . . well.'

> *'Oh . . .'*
> *Mam used to use that one, too.*
> *With work. Old boyfriends. Me.*
> *It was always a*
> *– headache, or*
> *– cold, or*
> *– upset tummy.*
> *I wait for Alice to give me*
> *another excuse to leave.*

'It's – um – it's difficult to explain.'

I think back to all the rehearsals of this conversation I've had, and they all jumble in my head.

'The Illness takes spoons, you see, and it means that I can't do things like run or – music – music is hard. And I need to spend a lot of time resting, and sometimes it means I disappear, although not entirely – I am in bed, after all. So . . .'

It's not coming out right. He looks away, far into the distance.

> *'You know, Alice,*
> *if you don't want to meet me,*
> *you can just say.'*

I watch the whites grow in my own eyes on screen.

'No! No, Rowan, it's not that. I'm not explaining myself very well. I do want to meet you. I want to run along the beach with you and go cycling and do a million different impossible –'

'So come do them, then!'
I'm shouting now.
I shouldn't, but
this really hurts.
Another person I love
making their excuses to
leave.

'I can't,' I say, my voice breaking. 'I want to, but the Illness –'

'I'm late picking up Jonah.'
I stand up and
K I C K
the stones
so they scatter.

'Rowan –'
A loud, high-pitched sound shrieks through my speakers and I clamp my hands over my ears.

My phone rings.
I glance at it,
ready to hurl another call from Dad
into the sea,

when I see who it is.

The sound stops and all I can see onscreen is his ear.

'Hello?'

I clutch my chest and try to slow my heartbeat. And, from my speakers, I hear a woman on the other end of the line.

'Rowan? I've been trying to get in touch with your mother –'

'She's not –
she's not available at the moment.
I told you that it was me who –'

'I really would prefer to speak –'

'I get it,
but you can't.
What's wrong?'
My heart hammers.

I hear a sigh from a long way away.

'There's a situation. You should come right away. And please – do get in touch with your mother, because this really is –'

Jonah Jonah Jonah.
I'm running.
Scrambling over stones.

The line breaks. There are stones and gulls and Rowan's breathing and it gets difficult to hear the woman on the other end of the phone.

But there's one thing I do hear. And judging by the way Rowan seems to

> stop

mid-stride, I think he heard it, too.

'Jonah has climbed to the top of the bell tower and we can't get him down.'

It's happened.
It's happened.
It's happened.

For one moment, I see a stretch of blue sky. Eyes trying to grab hold of something that isn't there.

And even though I'm the one that's sinking as he drops the phone from his ear – it looks very much like he's the one that is falling.

And I reach out my hand to grab him.

But I'm not there.

Call ended.

65

Alice

I throw my laptop to the end of the bed and lift myself out of it, so I'm standing in the middle of the floor.

My legs buckle and my head swirls until there's a monster screaming in my ear, and I know – I know – it's the Illness. And I've used the word 'bedbound' in meetings with hundreds of doctors over the last five years, but I've never felt so bound to this bed – like invisible ties are digging into my wrists and keeping me prisoner.

I lean against the wall and breathe. Breathe. Breathe. And then the door opens and they all tumble in.

Cecelia is smiling and I can see all the jokes about my date get lost on the way in as she sees me. Dad comes striding from behind her to grab me.

'Hey, hey, hey,' he says, guiding me back to bed.

'Rowan. Something – something's happened.'

Mum joins Dad and together they lay me back on the bed.

'What on earth –?'

I take a deep breath. 'Rowan's little brother. Something's happened. The bell tower.'

Cecelia swears and runs to the window from where you could just perhaps see a boy stuck at the very top of a tower in the distance. 'I can't see anything, but there are a load of people around . . . You think he's climbed it?'

I nod. 'He's up there. No one can get him down.'

Mum shakes her head. 'How'd he even get up there? They locked the door years ago.'

But it isn't locked any more, is it? I watched with Rowan as Charlie broke open the door, pulling off the handle. If they left it propped open, it would be easy for a little boy to slip in. And if the door slammed behind him, how would anyone be able to get it open again without a handle?

'There're some loose bricks up the side. They'd make pretty good handholds if you wanted to climb,' Cecelia says.

'How old is this kid?' Dad asks. 'I can't see him climbing –'

This is all wasting time and I dig my palms into the mattress and try to lift myself up again, but I'm too out of breath. And I feel like punching my pillow because, in any other body, I'd be running out of the door, stomping into shoes and climbing that tower with my bare hands.

Cecelia is watching me. She bends down, her strong fingers gripping my knee.

'I can do it,' she whispers as Mum and Dad talk.

I shake my head. 'No. No, it's too dangerous –'

'Not for me. Al – I climb every day. I don't need a door to get up there. I can just zip up, real quick, check he's all right and then wait with him until –'

'NO,' I say.

'They should have knocked that thing down years ago – it's not safe,' Mum says to Dad over by the window, oblivious to what Cecelia is talking about doing. 'Last time I saw it, the steps were crumbling away and there was a chunk of wall missing that anyone could come tumbling out of . . .'

We all turn our heads to the window, looking for falling dots in the distance.

My heart is in my ears. And all I can think about is Rowan. Rowan as he got that call. The look on his face. The way his eyes just emptied. This isn't just a boy stuck up a tower. This is his brother moments away from falling to his death all over again.

Cecelia is still looking at me and she can see my resolve crumbling. She turns to Dad.

'Jayce – you got a spare one of those strap thingies?'

'Just for my GoPro, but you can use that on my account if you want. Thinking about streaming something, are you?'

They bustle about and no one sees me shaking my head. Sitting by as another person bypasses a red light and goes hurtling towards something inevitably bad – all as I watch, helplessly, from my bed.

But this isn't just about breaking a commute record, is it? This is Jonah. This is Rowan.

Dad helps Cecelia strap the camera over her shoulders. She looks impossibly strong, standing with her feet planted hip-width apart like a superhero ready to take flight, her fists clenched and her eyes narrowed.

'You're all set,' Dad says.

Cecelia looks at me. 'I can do this,' she mouths.

And – looking at her – I almost think she can. She turns on her heel and runs out of the room. I hear her thunder down the stairs, into her shoes and out of the door.

'Where's she off to?' Dad says.

I open my laptop slowly. 'She's going to climb the tower.'

Dad swears and runs to the window. Mum pinches her lips, keeping back words.

And I know. I know those words. Because they're the same words that are going through my mind, too.

I open Screen Cast. And I see Dad's camera online.

And, as I click it, I think, *What have I done?*

66

daddycool-007

And now I am running. Faster than I ever have in my life.

The camera jumps and jerks, and I see flashes of glitter nails as Cecelia throws her arms out as if she's parting the air like water. Her shoes slap on the tarmac and her breath chugs out of her, and I'm reminded of the time she called me from the middle of a park run – only this time I can't speak to her. I can't tell her, *Be careful. Please. Please.*

She rounds the corner and the prison-bar school looms into view, packed with a crowd of parents and children, their eyes all on the tower. And I hunt for Rowan in the sea of blurry faces, but I can't see him. Not with the group of teachers huddled together. Or waiting on the street for the police or the fire brigade to arrive. Or even with the thicket of men trying to ram open the handle-less door to the bell tower.

'Idiots,' Cecelia pants. '"Oh, look at me, I'm a big strong man. I can use my FISTS to break down this giant metal door."'

She pushes through the crowd of people and among them I recognize Charlie and Fran looking guiltily at the tower, no crowbar in sight, but also no Rowan. Where is he?

Cecelia runs round the building and the noise from the crowd disappears.

'Where's she going?' says Dad.

But then she stops, taking a moment to steady her breathing and wipe her hands down her clothes. One leg lifts up and she uses her feet to pull herself on top of a big red bin.

'Are those my trainers?' Mum tuts.

But we're up. On to the bin and then quickly up the drainpipe and on to the roof of the school, as easy as breathing.

'Something tells me she's done that before,' Dad says.

She jogs across the black roof – avoiding puddles and lost balls – towards the tower jutting up from the side of the building towards the clouds. And, as she gets close, I see what Mum meant about the building being old.

It's falling down. Disintegrating. Chipped bricks balance on cracked cement, with gaps where others have fallen away altogether. Cecelia dusts her hands again and we look up with her at the clouds, where the top of the tower looms.

'I've always wanted to do this.'

She puts out her hand, pushes her fingers into a hole and pulls herself up.

My heart has jumped into my throat and I've reached out for Mum's hand without even thinking about it.

Cecelia looks down, slotting her foot into an impossibly small crack. The camera grates against the wall as she pulls herself up again. And again. And we hear her breathing get jagged – almost like she's laughing.

'Please say you're recording this,' she pants.

I hear Dad scratching his stubble. 'She's actually bonkers, that one.'

She climbs and climbs. Moving her arms and legs into places where I didn't even see holes. And the camera is pointed towards the brick, so there's no way of knowing how high she's got other than the occasional glimpse of bright sky getting closer and closer.

And then, far away, we hear a shout. 'There's a girl climbing up the side!'

The crowd erupts. And I think I hear people shouting at her to stop. To come down. Praying and swearing and screaming.

Cecelia laughs. 'Oh, shut up. It's *fine*.'

She reaches up to grab another brick. And, for one heart-lurching second, I think she's got it. That she can do this. That she's impossibly strong. But then we watch as the brick is dislodged from the wall, coming off in her hand. And on the screen it's almost like a cartoon – where the coyote catches an anvil and for a moment just hangs in the air, confused about what just happened.

But then I hear the intake of breath. See the scramble of her body. Feel my heart for one moment

stop.

The screen splinters, bricks now scratching at the lens. Mum has turned away and Dad has run to the window and I'm just sitting and screaming silently – again and again – as my friend falls

falls

falls.

My insides lurch and crack and disintegrate like ancient brick. And all I can think about is how – again – I'm watching helplessly as another friend dies.

But suddenly the scrabbling stops and we swing out with her body, so the world below spins. Then her hand stretches out and clamps on to a brick.

'She's got it. She's got it!' Dad shouts in my ear. Mum's hands are shaking against mine..

'Holy . . .' Cecelia gasps.

We look up with her – at her fingers holding her weight. She lets out her breath.

'Sorry, sorry,' she says. 'Don't freak out, Al. I'm fine – just missed a hold. We're good, we're good . . .'

Her voice sounds like music, and adrenaline rains from my shoulders in thick drops.

She's slower now, but she's still climbing steadily. And soon the broken roof of the tower swings into view and she's scrambling up, out and over the broken wall to the platform at the top.

I let out a breath I very much knew I was holding.

'Legend!' Dad shouts, clapping.

'Idiot,' Mum says, rubbing her chest.

Cecelia lies on the floor for a moment, panting. And then a small voice comes from behind her.

'Why did you come up the side?'

She rolls over and lifts herself so she's sitting with her back to the world below and staring into the dark tunnel of stairs disappearing under the floor. And looking at her, picking at the wall, is a boy with bright blond hair.

'Jonah, right?' Cecelia says.

He nods.

My eyes comb him for bumps and bruises and my ribs seem to crack when I see that he's fine. He's fine. He's fine.

I pick up my phone.

> Jonah's okay! Cecelia climbed up the
> side of the tower. She's with him now.
> I can see him. He's fine. I promise,
> he's fine x

I send the message with trembling fingers and watch as Cecelia puts out her hand to shake Jonah's.

'I'm Cecelia. But you can just call me Spiderwoman.'

Jonah's eyes widen. 'Can I climb up the side, too?'

Cecelia stands up. 'That, little man, is the dumbest thing I've ever heard anyone say. Climb the side of a building? No way. Real heroes use the stairs – come on.'

The screen gets darker as she takes his hand and leads him down the stairs, and we hear him asking questions and her telling him to watch out for holes.

And then there's another voice. A light shines into the camera and, behind it, a man in a bright firefighter suit shouts, 'Are there any others?'

'Nope,' Cecelia says. 'Just us. We're both okay, aren't we, pal?'

'Are you a fireperson?' Jonah asks.

They tumble down the steps and the light from outside illuminates a mangled door and a figure pulling away from the grip of a police officer and running through the door.

'Jonah? Jonah!'

And I can't see his face. But I'd know that voice anywhere.

My heart lurches as Rowan grabs hold of his brother and pulls him out of the building, frantically checking him for injuries, his phone still in his hand.

'Are you okay? Are you okay? What were you – why would you – don't ever do that again! Don't ever –' He holds on to him. Tight.

Teachers and firefighters and teenagers I vaguely recognize swarm round Cecelia, blocking my view.

'You were so amazing.'

'What's your name again?'

I crane forward to see through the arms of people slapping her on the back and checking out her hands and arms. I spot the same smartly dressed woman Rowan met at school the first time we talked. With her are the police.

An officer taps him on the shoulder until he lets go of Jonah. She takes Jonah's hand, says something to Rowan and almost seems to gently push him away.

He turns towards us for a moment and I can see his expression. And it's as if the world has drained around him. He glances at Jonah. He rubs his face. And he runs.

You have disconnected from this stream.

67

Alice

Mum and Dad are talking, so, for a moment, they don't notice me muster all the spoons I have and lift myself out of bed.

My blood fizzes and erupts and I can almost see the droplets like dark shadows in my eyes. I lunge for the wall.

'Alice!' Mum says, leaping up to hold me. 'What are you –'

'Rowan,' I say. 'Rowan needs me. I need to go and find –'

'Don't be silly,' she says, pushing me back towards the bed.

I try to fight her, but I can't. Sitting down again feels like coming up for air, but my thoughts are still drowning.

'He ran. He ran away. His eyes – they must know. The police must know about his mum. He needs me and –'

'Why don't you call him, kiddo?' Dad says, handing me my phone. 'Maybe he's just gone for a walk to clear his head.'

But Dad didn't see his eyes. Didn't see the slight push on his chest from the police officer. Doesn't know just what's at stake for Rowan and his brother if the police have found out that his parents are no longer around.

I pick up my phone, though. And I dial his number just like last time, when he turned away from me and thought that I didn't care enough to meet him.

I close my eyes and press call.

68

Rowan

My phone screams at me.
Alice.
My thumb
HOVERS
over the green answer button.
But what would I say?
What are the words for?
I fucked everything up
and
I thought I could protect him, but I
can't
can't
can't.
How can I look into the eyes of someone else
who wants to leave me
and tell her that
she's right.
Alice. Mum.
Even Jonah.
They're better off without me.

Call declined.

69

Alice

The line goes dead and I come alive. I stand up.

Mum keeps her hands round my wrists.

'Alice – this is stupid. You can't do it. Your dad can go out and try to find him, but you –'

'No!' I shout, and the words stop even Manta. 'I'm going. Me. Me in this body. And I know it's broken and I don't need you to remind me of that, thank you. But Rowan's my friend and my friend is in trouble and I can't just stand by and watch this time, Mum – I can't! Not like with Cecelia. Not like with – Wesley.'

His name haunts the room. And I see the thoughts pass across their faces like shadows – how I sat in my bed and watched him die. How I couldn't cry out or stop it from happening.

But not this time. Not with Rowan. He needs to know that I'm here for him. That even when everyone else leaves – his dad, his mum – I stay. I'm here.

I wrench my arm away and Mum steps back, looking shaken. 'I can't,' she says. 'You can't. It's too dangerous.'

And I know that she's seeing into my tomorrow, when all my spoons will be buried. But, right now, my tomorrow isn't quite as important.

'I'm going,' I say. 'You can't stop me.'

Mum throws up her hands and turns away. But Dad smiles, sadly, clearing his throat so he sounds almost normal, even if he doesn't look it.

'We're not your jailers, Alice. If you're going – then go.'

Mum slides him a look like poison, but I nod.

I muster all the spoons I have and step. Forward. Forward. And I can almost hear the clink as the spoons drop at my feet. The Illness roars in my ears and I clutch the door frame, looking out at the landing to the impossible number of stairs.

And I want to smash things. I want to punch holes in the walls. I want to rip, tear, squeeze and throw off the weights that are holding my body down and float away into a world where what I want to do and what I can do are the same thing.

But instead I just quiver against the wall and turn back to Dad, who's looking at me with eyes that feel every last bit of pain I do.

'I need – help. Please,' I say.

Mum shakes her head, looking out of the window towards the bell tower. Dad rubs his neck, his hands shaking. And I've never seen him like this and it's breaking my heart, but I need to do this.

I need to.

He steps forward. 'Of course. Of course we'll help. We'll always help. Won't we, Sophia?'

Mum makes a noise like she's choking.

My heart sings as Dad puts my arm over his shoulder. 'Thank you. Thank you,' I pant.

Mum spins round and I can see her eyes glistening. And *I'm sorry I'm sorry I'm sorry* for upsetting her. For adding to the worry she already carries. But also I perhaps feel more Alive than I ever have done before.

Dad lifts me up and manoeuvres me forward. And, with his help, I walk. Down the stairs.

Dad huffs and winces as he stubs his toe on the skirting board, but he doesn't let me go. And I concentrate on moving my legs down, down, and it feels a bit like falling and flying all at once.

And there's the phone table, with the stack of magazines. And there's the kitchen, with pots piled in the sink. And there are three pairs of shoes by the front door and not one of them is mine.

Mum scurries round me, her lips tight. She takes out a pair of old trainers from the cupboard that are barely worn, and I know are mine, but they don't seem to fit me any more.

'Just wear these,' Dad says, kicking Cecelia's sandals over.

I slide them on to my feet. And I can feel the leather where it's been worn from her running round the park. I can feel the miles they have stepped in, and the heights they've climbed. And I feel like I'm Living all of that by just being upright in my hallway.

Mum puts on my sunglasses and my earplugs and my coat. And then she opens the front door and I see outside.

Birds. Cars. People planting flowers in boxes outside their homes. And one of them stops to look over at me and maybe wonders who the girl in dark glasses is who's stepping out into the world.

And it's Me.

Alice.

Alive.

And now I'm outside, in the world. For real this time. I feel wind on my bare legs and the concrete path under my shoes and the sunlight burning my eyes, even with the glasses on. And it's wonderful and horrible and I want to keep moving and I want to go back and I want to laugh and cry and scream and dance, but it's all I can do to keep breathing.

There are hands holding me up. Opening car doors. Sliding me inside a car seat that's so far reclined it probably isn't even legal any more.

And now I'm in a car. A car that smells hot, with stitched seats that scratch my thighs. And it feels like going back in time, to a place where speed ruled and the wind knew my face.

Dad pauses just for a moment, hand on the door. And I know he's remembering the last time I was in a car and how much it hurt me. And I know he's feeling as if he's the one doing that to me, but he isn't. I am. I'm making this decision and it's bad and entirely right.

'It's okay,' I say. 'Just hurry.'

He nods and it's strange to see him not making jokes. He closes the door and comes round to start the engine. 'Where are we going?'

For a moment, I don't know. Where is Rowan? How can I be there for him when I don't know where 'there' is? But then there's only one place he would go to hide.

'The playground behind the school,' I say.

I close my eyes and shove the earplugs as deep into my ears as they can go. And I slide on the pair of unplugged headphones Mum is handing me from the back seat, too.

Dad pulls out of the drive and I grip the door. He isn't making his usual celebrity jokes about my sunglasses and I think he's perhaps as afraid as I am.

I concentrate on my breathing, and try to remember what it was like to ride a bike with Wesley. And how all I could do then was watch him die, but how this time I'm reaching out. I'm stopping that car in its tracks. I'm rewriting all of it.

I scrunch my face up and try not to feel the spoon-annihilating noise still piercing through the headphones, and the flashing lights and the rumbling under my fingers, and try to keep the cracks together as my world seems to earthquake.

A short car ride = 3 spoons

I peel an eye open and I recognize the tall green gates of the school from when I sat on the bench with Rowan. And Dad drives round and round, trying to find a space, until he looks at me and decides to just pull over on a double yellow line close to the fire engines still parked outside the school.

He turns off the engine and Mum takes off my headphones.

'Are you okay?' She sounds shaken, so I steady myself for her.

'I'm fine. Let's just get out.'

They spill round the outside of the car and, for a split second, I'm alone. And I use it to take a deep breath.

I can feel the Illness racing through spoons, but it hasn't taken all of me yet. And – impossibly – I'm outside, sitting in a car in front of the school. I'm not strapped to the chest of someone else. I'm not pretending their life is my own.

I am Living. With a capital L. And I'm choosing Rowan.

My door opens and I'm carefully manoeuvred out. My arm gets stuck in the seat belt and I'm running my own race now to stand up – blinking off the darkness that's patching in, and breathing in air I know is there, but that I can't. Quite. Catch.

I feel cold whispers on my toes and sandals digging into my feet in strange places. I can hear the cries of seagulls carried on the same breeze that I am, and I wonder if – just like them – I could jump on its back and fly.

Dad looks round and winces. 'There's no way we can get there in the car. We're going to have to walk.'

Mum starts laughing, but in a way that doesn't really sound like she finds anything funny at all. 'You've got to be kidding me.'

My insides swoop with gratitude for him and I clutch his arm harder. 'There's a path behind the school. It leads through a tunnel and then round into a playground. There's a climbing frame . . .'

I know because I've walked it with Rowan.

I can see Mum shaking her head out of the corner of my eye, because I might as well have said that it's all the way in China for all the spoons I have to walk there, when I can feel them dropping just standing here and being outside and having to argue.

I'm still here, though. I don't know for how much longer, but I am.

'We need to hurry,' I gasp.

Dad looks at Mum and they share something and I'm not sure what it is. But it makes Mum sigh heavily and let go of my arm, as Dad reaches down and picks me up in his arms, like he's rescuing me from a burning building and I can feel the flames at my ankles.

'I can't watch,' she says, and she turns away with her hand to her face, and it's like watching someone crash into something entirely real and unmovable while not moving at all.

She crumbles. And I can't do anything, because Dad has started to move – one step in front of the other – away from her. But I see her face in the wing mirror and her eyes are on me, anyway.

We circle the green gates of the school and I peer through the bars as they flicker past. And, like an old film, I see people crowded round Cecelia and her smile bursting like a flare.

'She'll be popular after this,' Dad says, between deep, rusty breaths.

My heart leaps a little, and I don't know if it's because I'm pleased for her, or if I'm worried that she might not have time for me any more.

Dad starts wheezing and his footsteps become heavier.

'Do you need a rest?' I ask.

'Not – yet.'

We round the school, and the people and the tower disappear in a haze behind us, and now we're faced with a busy road, with cars hurtling past like bullets. But there's a path winding round dehydrated trees and brown plants and tunnelling into an underpass.

We walk down the hill and Dad's steps become hurried and more desperate.

And then we're in the tunnel and it's so dark that I can hardly see with my sunglasses on. And I'm not sure if we're going forward or back, or if we're just caught together in a frozen black sea.

Dad falters. 'Just – one –'

His arms shake and buckle as he lowers me down on to a bench in the middle of the tunnel. The backrest has been broken off, so I lie with my legs curled instead, and take off my glasses.

'Are you okay?' I keep my hand on his arm and feel my muscles taking spoons.

He's red-faced and breathing heavily, but he smiles, kneeling on the ground next to me. 'I really need to get back to tae kwon do – I'm never going to get my black belt in this shape, eh?'

He pinches his belly and I try to make my arm pat his shoulder, but it doesn't seem to want to move.

I take a deep breath. Just a little more. Just a little longer. Just a bit.

And then Dad bends, and behind him I see it – rising from an impossible place and stretching its limbs over the concrete towards me. The kraken.

My breath catches. It's beautiful. Just as beautiful as when I first saw it through the eyes of the artist who brought it to life. And – even through my own eyes – it's just as strong. Just as vibrant and powerful and able as it was before.

I can see the thousand brushstrokes, and the patience and attention to detail he needed to create it. I can see the way the purples slowly melt into blues and greens and yellows, so the light seeping in from the end of the tunnel might be rippling across its body as it bursts out of its cage. And here – in real, beautiful Life – the kraken is not confined to the concrete. It's not trapped inside the walls. It's free.

Dad stretches up. 'You ready?'

'Yes,' I say. And I mean it.

70

Alice

And now I have my sunglasses back on as we're climbing out of the tunnel and walking up a path to the children's playground. And the sun is hurdling over clouds to keep up, making shadows jump and tangle across flower beds and trees.

It's beautiful.

Dad walks on and on with me in his arms and I'm not sure his rest did anything to help at all. I want to get down and walk with him for a while – perhaps let him lean on me to get his breath back – but all my body can do is hold on to him, and even that's becoming harder.

Being outside. Clinging on to consciousness. This is my uphill climb.

We get to the end of the path and I can see the slide and the fireman's pole now, jutting down from the castle standing tall in the middle of the playground. And I know Rowan is in there and I know that if I can just reach him –

Dad coughs and falters and – for one moment – I slip.

And I can't do anything about it. He's dropping me and desperately trying not to, but he's not quite strong enough and neither am I.

We're so close. So close. But we're falling. Together. And it's over and I'm not going to make it, and the weight of that feels heavier still.

But then, from under me, hands.

'Okay, there we go, there we go.'

Dad and I both turn at the same time and see her beside us. Sharing the weight.

'You took your bloody time,' Dad gasps, rearranging his grip on me.

Mum purses her lips.

'You came,' I say.

'Let's just get this over with quickly, okay?'

They carry me between them. And the path feels less bumpy and my thoughts can clear for a moment and I can look towards the climbing frame and think about what it is that I'm going to say to him.

Because, if I'm honest, I don't know. I just know that I need to say something. Do something.

We step on to the soft black sponge of the playground.

We walk past the deserted roundabout and the empty swings.

We stumble across the hopscotch.

And then we're at the steps to the castle climbing frame. Where once I saw long, strong fingers grab the rusted handles and pull us up. This time, I reach out and see my own.

And I might not have the spoons to grab them and pull myself up, but I have brilliant, wonderful parents to lift me.

They slide me on to the castle floor and the wooden slats feel like sandpaper. I press my back against the wall and feel its coldness through my dress like an icy puddle. I grip on as tightly as my hands will allow and try to remember to breathe.

But it's hard to do that. Because there – in front of me – head in his hands.

Is Rowan.

71

Alice and Rowan

And now I am here. Seeing Rowan whole – from his fists clutching the roots of his hair, through the bend of his body, to his torn trainers stomping on the mermaid.

I see him. I see him and my whole body seems to spark to life and splutter out in one go.

> *I bury my head.*
> *Usually if I ignore people,*
> *they eventually go away.*
> *I need this stranger to*
> *get lost*
> *before I lose myself.*

I breathe. Breathe.
'Thanks, Dad.'
He slides a look at Rowan before asking me, 'You okay?'
'I'm fine,' I breathe. 'Could you give us a moment?'

> *My heart is hammering.*
> *Go away. Go away. Go away.*

I feel as if I'm
burning.
Imploding like a dying star.
And now there are
E Y E S
watching me melt down.

'I'll be over with your mum,' Dad says.

He flashes Rowan another suspicious look and moves away to sit on the nearby bench with Mum.

And then it's just him and me. Alice and Rowan. Together.

He's not looking at me, so I take a moment to breathe and pick through my words.

'Rowan? I'm here.'

I wrench my head up, expecting
– the headteacher
– social services
– the police
ready to ask the questions that will
take Jonah away from me for good.
But instead I see a real-life
ghost girl
pressed against the wall like she's
keeping it up.
'Alice?'
My guts roller-coaster
and I'm not sure which feeling to pick out

305

through the stabbing guilt in me and
the hope in her smile.
I shake my head. 'What are you doing here?'

He knows me. He knows me in this body even though it's slipping through the slats in the floor.

And even though I can feel his pain radiating from him like a fever, the world has never seemed a more beautiful place.

'You told me once that this was where you escaped to.'

I drag my fingers through my hair.
'Look, I need to be alone right now, Alice.
I need you to –'

'Leave?'

He slides a look at me. For a moment, our eyes meet, and I feel my heart skip.

I smile. 'I'm not leaving, Rowan.'

My gut wrenches because
this is what I chose for myself, isn't it?
Her.
Her over Jonah.
And I can feel myself still wanting to
choose her again,
despite everything.

He doesn't take his hands from his hair.

'Why did you run?'

> I turn away.
> You saw.
> You sent me that text.
> I said I'd protect Jonah
> and I didn't.
> I was late picking him up
> and then he climbed that tower
> and now the social are asking questions
> and they're going to –'
> My words choke.
> The whole world is crumbling out from under me.
> And I can't get
> how the floor I'm sitting on
> hasn't moved.

I want to reach out and put my arms round him, but they don't seem to want to move.

'It wasn't your fault.'

> It was. It was. It WAS.
> I feel the guilt tsunami-ing
> up through my bones,
> making my fist
> THUMP
> on the castle floor
> so the whole thing finally starts
> earthquaking.

I jump and dart a look down at Dad, who's staring up and trying to pretend that he isn't.

'Rowan – it isn't your fault. It isn't. You weren't there. You couldn't have stopped him from climbing –'

> *'Exactly!' I spit.*
> *'I wasn't there, was I?'*
> *I'm shouting and I can't stop.*
> *Just – go away, Alice.*
> *I need to think.'*
> *I put my head in my hands.*

His voice is splitting spoons, but I'm clinging on.

'You can be there for someone without being present,' I say quietly. But the n – if that's true – what on earth am I doing in the middle of a children's playground, as my parents huddle together on a bench waiting to scrape what's left of me off the floor?

I turn to him. Now his feet and hands are planted on the floor, like he might spring up at any moment, his hair out of its band now and wild. And he has holes in his shoes and dirt on his hands and a mad look in his eyes – but I know him. I know him like he and I are the same.

'You don't have to do this alone.'

> *She's just not getting it.*
> *'Alice,' I sigh.*
> *Just – you don't understand, okay?*
> *You've got –'*
> *I wave my hand at the*

                    people huddled on the bench.
          Careers lady. The bloke she called Dad.
                        'My dad walked out.
        The shit with Mam got too hard and he
                            chose himself.
            Over her. Over me. Over Jonah.
                            And Mam –'
                I spit the thought from my head
                        like an abscess.
                    '– she'd hold her own kid
            off the side of a bell tower.'

My breath gutters and I try to concentrate on how solid the
floor feels under my hand.

'Have you told your dad that things got worse?'

                            I shake my head.
                        'He doesn't care.
            No one cares about kids like us, Alice.'

I look up. To the sky.
    'I care.'

                    'I fucked it up,' I whisper.
            'I thought I could protect him, but
                I'm just as bad as Dad.'

He's not listening to me. And I don't know how many words
I have left.

                                309

'If you told him – your dad – if you told him the truth, he could help you. And Fran. Charlie. My mum. If you told them, they could help.'

I failed.
I failed.
I failed.

He pinches his eyes and I see the same worry lines on his face that I see on mine in the mirror, always hiding what we are. What we're really feeling. Always pretending that we're stronger than we are, when sometimes – sometimes – we perhaps aren't.

And it's okay, isn't it? It's okay to show someone that you're disappearing. Especially if that helps them find their own lines.

'Rowan. Rowan – I'm not . . . I'm not well.'

I rub my face.
'Ask your parents to help you, Alice.'

And the fog finally catches up. It licks my toes like flames.

'I do.' I gasp. 'Not with words, but I ask them. I ask them to – to get me out of bed in the morning. I ask them to feed me. Worry for me. Keep me from falling over in the middle of my bedroom and pick me up whenever I do.'

I turn back.
'What are you –?'
But then I see her.
See her in a way that feels like

waking up.

> *Alice.*
> *Her twig-thin arms.*
> *Her ghost-white face.*
> *Her eyes leaking light.*
> *But still somehow smiling.*
> *'What – Alice?'*

The fog swirls higher and the light dips lower and Rowan reaches out and grabs me. Grabs me by the hand.

And our skin. Our skin together. Him and me. Both. It's one of many impossible things a girl who is bound but boundless can have.

I look at his eyes. Dark marbles.

I can't clutch his hand back, but I focus on how it feels to have him

> reach out through the world between us
> and hold me.

'I'm ill, Rowan,' I whisper.

> *Alice. Alice. Alice.*
> *I stumble closer to her.*
> *'Alice –'*
> *Why does she look like she's*
> *fading away?*

His skin feels impossibly cold.

'No more hiding. No more lies.'

I tilt my head. To the sky. Feel the last dregs of sun.

Then I look at him. The crease above his eyes. If I had spoons, I would thumb-iron that away.

'It's time to let people see, Rowan.'

Oh shit.
Oh shit.
She's sinking away
into depths I
can't reach.
I reach out,
try to grab her back.
'Alice?
Alice!'

Hello.

That's my name.

Or perhaps it was.

No matter.

I came.

I climbed.

And I told him.

I just hope.

I just hope.

This time.

He listened.

'H-help!'

72

And now

I am

lost.

73

Alice

Beep.
    Hands.
Beep.
    Whispers.
Beep.
    Words.
Beep.
    'Alice?'
Beep.
    Me.
Beep.
    ME.
Beep.
    I am here.
Beep.
    In between these heartbeats.
Beep.
    I want to tell them.
Beep.
    I want to show them.

Beep.

I am HERE.

Beep.

But the beeps.

Beep.

For now.

Beep.

Are doing that for me.

74

Alice

Days and days and days of endless, burning fog.

And then. In patches. It clears.

Wires.

Crossing and cartwheeling. Down from a bag of clear liquid and needling into my arm.

Eyes.

Not ones I know, but crinkled kindly and staring at me from over a green paper mask. And then a mask of my own is hooked on to my face. One that smells of plastic and hisses with sea breeze.

It will make me better. It will stop some of the pain.

Hands.

Mum's hands. Holding mine. And Dad's footsteps pacing the floor.

'She's never been this bad before, Sophia.'

Mum's eyes see mine through the fog.

'She's on her way back.'

I am.

75

Alice

At first I want to ask how long.

How long have I been in hospital? With the spoon-destroying strip lights and the incessant beeping and the questions, questions.

And then I want to ask about Rowan.

Did he hear me?

Did he reach out and ask for help?

And then I want to ask what happened.

What happened when he saw who I was?

Did he at least look back when he walked away?

But I don't have the spoons for words. I barely have enough to form any thoughts at all.

But I have enough to cartwheel patterns on my eyelids as I try to stay perfectly still and let my body fight whatever part of the Illness has made it fall so spectacularly backwards.

I let the light splatter into giant paintings of krakens. Of mermaids. Of a family of humpback whales, back together again.

In my mind, I strap myself to the arms of paintbrushes and I create whole worlds of light. And I will the ink to seep down through my bones, into my veins and deep into my cells. To paint in something new. Something working. Something beautiful.

And I prepare myself. Because I know that when my body is back again, I have a whole new world to step into. And for that I'm going to need something special.

Not my streamers. Not Rowan. Not even Mum and Dad.

I'm going to need Alice. Because, when it comes to capital-L Living, she's all I've got.

76

Alice

It almost seems impossible, but I've made a new friend.

I didn't know her name for a few days. Just the kind crinkle of her eyes. The wink she gave me when she was saying something I couldn't quite understand, but which made me feel that, whatever it was, it was something nice. But then I caught a glimpse of her nametag – three letters that it took spoons and spoons to read, but that eventually detangled themselves in my head and became a word.

May.

May wears blue scrubs and a gold necklace round her neck with a coin on it. She wears glitter on her eyelids, and when she leans over to check the beeping by my bed she smells like the inside of a dressing room on the set of a Hollywood film.

I can't tell May my name because I can't make my lips move. But she seems to know it anyway and whispers secrets in my ear like we're old friends.

Sometimes she tells jokes. And hours after she's gone, when the lights have been turned low and I can gather the spoons to wake up, the jokes tumble into pictures and I laugh.

And somehow, days and days and days later, May is there suddenly, whispering to me about Mum and Dad, and the words sink in like quicksand.

'Don't tell your dad, Alice, but your mum messed with him when he was asleep just now.'

Words. Words I understand. And I can slide my eyes to the left in time to see Dad stretching – his own glitter eyeshadow brightening his face. And somewhere inside I laugh.

May sees. And her face cracks into a smile that shows beautiful gapped teeth.

'There you are,' she says. 'I see you.'

77

Alice

I'm being discharged.

Away from the impossibly bright lights, and the beeping, and the people who became my friends. Away from the questions we can't answer, and they can't, either.

Mum isn't crying this time, though. And the bags they have wired into my veins have been drip-feeding spoons and gluing the lines back together between Me and my body.

And as I'm wheeled out with my sunglasses on and my earplugs in, I hunt for May in the faces wishing me luck, and find her hand.

'You stay away this time, you hear me?' she says.

'I'll try,' I promise.

I grip her hand as tightly as I can before letting her float away, wishing on her like she's a shooting star. I don't ever want to come back.

I'm wheeled down long corridors with art on the walls so colourful I can't look at it. But the colours stay with me as I'm led outside and into the car. As the silent headphones go back round my ears. And I take my last look at the world – at Mum and Dad swirling with colours – as I know the car will take the spoons that I've slowly built up enough for them to let me go home. But I'll get them back again. Slowly – they'll come back.

The car roars.

Colour stretches.

Then the smell of home.

A whirlwind fish spinning in his tank.

The sigh of a duvet in a puff of chalk.

Lights off. World dulls. But the colours stay with me.

I close my eyes and swim.

78

Alice

I'm dreaming and I'm swimming.

The water is warm and clear, like a bath. At the bottom, coral twists out from the jagged seabed and reaches its fingers towards me. But I'm too far away for it to touch me.

And I barrel-roll on to my back and look up, to where the sunlight is shattering into beams and where, up on the surface, there are legs paddling.

Cecelia. Mum. Dad.

Rowan.

I'm too far down to reach them. But I don't spin or kick to get to them this time, because I'm clinging to every spoon I have. And I wait for my last breath to gutter, and my lungs scream at me to *kick kick kick*, but I don't. I steady myself. And I take a lungful of water instead.

And the water doesn't taste like drowning. My lungs stop screaming and my body sighs and I feel the oxygen flowing through me as if my bones are breathing, too.

I reach up to my neck and there, cut into the sides, are gills. Gills to breathe the in-between.

And now – here – it's peaceful. It's warm. I can hear the chattering of surface sounds above and the tapping of hidden things below. And I don't belong in either place.

But I get the feeling that here – in the middle – I'm not alone.

'Alice?'

I open my eyes and it's Dad. He's swum down to see me.

'Hi,' I say, and I duck and dive, because I said a word. Even after the car took them from me again, I said a word out loud.

Dad's smile twinkles. 'Welcome back, kiddo.'

He swims away again and leaves a curious sight behind him. It almost seems like grains of my dream have been kicked up into reality, and my bedroom has been swept away into an ocean of blues.

I blink. But it doesn't shift. And trying to understand feels like trying to turn over an elephant in my mind.

Working out what's going on with the real world = 1 spoon

I let it trickle in slowly.

The swirling colour frosted over my walls.

The forest of deep-green coral gathered round Manta's tank and housing flashing starfish, shoals of yellow-tipped fish and the dead-eyed mouth of an eel lying in wait.

And, above me, a whole tunnel of water bursting round a light bulb and rippling as a gigantic manta ray comes sweeping over my bed.

My walls. My bedroom walls. They've been washed away. Taken by a wave. Replaced with an entire ocean of everything.

I reach out.

Taking Dad's hand = 1 spoon

'I've got to hand it to him. He might be a teenage delinquent, but he sure can paint.'

Rowan.

His name dips and dives and pulls at a thread of something that is attached to my ribs, my ears, the very tips of my toes. And I want to grab it and push it away. And it's painful and wonderful. And it's real and so entirely like a dream.

He has painted my bedroom walls. Every single bit of them.

He has dissolved them into our tunnel under the sea, and I want to lie on the floor with him and look up at the world and take his hand and –

Be.

I look around for him.

'When you're better, kiddo. He wants to see you, too.'

He wants to see me. Even after he saw me for who I was, he wants to see me.

And I wonder if anything else could ever feel quite as much like capital-L Living.

79

Alice

My spoons are back.

Perhaps not all-the-way back yet, but enough for me to sit up between Mum, Dad and Cecelia as we watch the recording of her on the local news the other week.

A reporter in a smart suit stands outside the school gates – in the same place I stood just a short while ago – and I wonder if he can see the ghost of my footprints.

Cecelia groans when she flashes on the screen, staring straight into the camera like it's a high-speed train hurtling towards her.

'Oh God, this is mortifying.'

'Shhh-shush! You're speaking over the best bit.' Dad turns the volume up loud.

'I'm joined now by the young rescuer, Cecelia Adebayo. Cecelia – what was going through your mind when you climbed that bell tower?'

The on-screen Cecelia's eyes bulge as the camera zooms in and there's a terrifying silence for a moment, which the real Cecelia wails through and tries to snatch the remote away from Dad.

'Turn – it – off!'

'Um – I dunno really. Just that it was quite high.'

'"Just that it was quite high",' Mum and Dad mock before falling over laughing.

I shake my head. 'I don't think I've ever seen you lost for words.'

'It's the camera, okay! It – it threw me.'

Mum and Dad continue to laugh at her, but over it I'm trying to listen. Because now, standing on-screen, is Jonah. Yellow-haired and waving into the camera like he's seeing me behind it again. And he's fine. He's fine.

'Shhh!' I say, and the others fall quiet. 'Let's listen.'

The reporter bends down to him. *Jonah, what were you doing all the way up the tower in the first place?*

He grins and there's that missing tooth. *I wanted to see the flowers.*

There are flowers all the way up there? the reporter asks.

Jonah shrugs. *My brother can make flowers out of nowhere, and big octopuses, too. He can do anything.*

The shot cuts to Rowan waving awkwardly at the camera while speaking to someone on the phone and my heart leaps. I want to pause it. Spend time looking at his long fingers and slanted smile. To look properly at his clothes – the same ones he was wearing when I saw him in real, technicolour life – like looking into a parallel universe where life carried on after mine stopped for a while – where my best friend was interviewed live on TV, and Rowan listened to me and walked back.

I can feel Cecelia's eyes on me, waiting to crack a joke, though, so I let the moment pass.

The reporter is back to Jonah now. *And are you pleased you were rescued?*

He sighs, like he's really trying to think about it. *'I could have got down on my own probably, because I got up there all by myself. But it was nice having Cecelia there, too – she makes me laugh.'*

On the screen, Jonah holds Cecelia's hand and Cecelia smiles in a strange, panicky way that shows her teeth.

This time, she manages to wrestle the remote away from Dad.

'Aaaaand delete. Honestly – that kid. Risked my neck going up to save him and the best thing he can say is that I cracked a couple of jokes up there.'

'Bet he couldn't get down fast enough,' Mum says, sliding away from Cecelia's hands as she tries to flick her.

But the reporter knows she did more than that, and we all do, too. So, when Mum and Dad leave, I use a spoon to hug her.

Hugging a hero = 1 spoon

'Thank you for saving him,' I say.

She pats my arm. 'You would've done the same if you could.'

'Have things got better now? With the others at school?'

She shrugs. 'I guess. A few people want to join the climbing club now, so at least it won't just be me and the creepy gym teacher. And Rowan's mates – Fran and Charlie – they've started inviting me to stuff, too, which beats eating on my own all the time. They're all right, actually. A bit gross, but all right.' She slides a look at me and hugs me tighter. 'None of them are a patch on you, though. And – by all accounts – you were off being your own hero that day, anyway.'

I bite my lip. I've been thinking about it and I'm wondering if that's true. Because however good it was to be there when

Rowan needed me, it was at the expense of so much more. Dad. Mum. And almost, nearly, me. Perhaps that's not entirely what being a hero is.

I turn to look at her. She has green in her hair now and she matches my walls. 'Do you know? Do you know if it worked? That he's okay?'

Cecelia grabs her phone and passes it to me. 'How about you let him tell you that himself?'

And on her phone are messages and messages and messages from Rowan.

Is she okay?

Dude – what's going on?

HELLO, ANSWER YOUR PHONE,
PLEASE.

Can I see her yet?

Please?

My fingers hover over the screen. And then I type.

You can come. Tomorrow.

Tomorrow.

80

Alice

I feel different inside these walls since they were painted.

It's not that they're not there, because they are. And I'm still here in this bed and I'm still battling the Illness and I'm not sure who's winning. It's more like I see them now. And I see that my life within these walls can be just like the sea. It can be dark. It can be wild. It can be uncertain and cold and can rip things away from me before I can reach in and claw them back.

But it can also be beautiful.

Since I rebuilt myself, I've been thinking a lot about being outside. At the time, it felt like I was Living – like I was putting my foot in the world and it would be worth all the bad for one moment of normal, where I could be there physically for someone who needed me.

But that's not Living any more, is it? My life as Alice isn't about climbing to great heights or pushing myself over my limit for one breath of borrowed air. For me, Living is breathing the in-between – creating wonderful worlds with my parents; laughing with Cecelia; and falling in love with a boy from my bed. Living is measured in spoons so I don't sink or swim to the surface.

So I can stop. And look. See beautiful things.

Mum pulls my bed up and asks me how I am, and this time I tell her the good and the bad. I tell her that the bones in my legs are burning again. I tell her that I'm worried about whether or not I will ever become a marine biologist. I tell her that I'm nervous about seeing Rowan.

But I also tell her that I love her. That I'm looking forward to whatever Dad has cooked up on the Cure Board for next week. And that really, right now at least, I'm happy.

She leans down and kisses me on the forehead, and I decide to tell her something else, too.

'Mum – I'm sorry that I'm Ill and that you had to give up your singing to look after me.'

She seems to fall into me for a moment, but when she lifts her head back again, her face is a smooth line. She cups my face in her hands.

'Never be sorry for that, Alice. Never.' Her eyes are storm-sky grey. 'You give me more joy than a hundred dance routines ever did.'

She traces her finger round the line of my smile.

'Don't you miss it, though? A little?'

She sighs and sits down on the bed. 'Sometimes – yes. Mainly just the other girls – they were a hoot.'

I take her hand. 'Maybe you could join a class or something? Have your own Cure Board day.'

She laughs. 'Your dad's crazy antics are enough for me.'

But I look at her. 'Seriously, though, Mum. Your life doesn't have to be just about me.'

She opens her mouth and I see the curve of a fake smile before she swallows it down. And then she leans over me, putting her lips on our fingers for a moment.

'I'll think about it. Although I love having you as my world, Alice – don't you forget it. You're not just a job to me, you know – you're also the strongest and most wonderful person.'

I smile until we both get a bit uncomfortable and she stands up, smoothing my bedspread under her hands.

'I do wish I could be more for you, though. If I could, I'd fill these walls full of people for you.'

I grimace. 'That sounds loud.'

'You know what I mean,' she says. 'People your age. Like you.'

She turns and carries on getting ready for work. But her words – they get me thinking.

I hadn't thought about there being others like me. Not the same age, but those trapped inside walls. Others that are still here, in this in-between, or ducking up from seabed to surface and wondering how to float. Or whether or not they even want to float – or just keep swimming, any way they can, to the surface.

Mum leaves for work, so I open my laptop and connect to Stream Cast.

Welcome back to Stream Cast, Alice

Users online:

No one is online yet – why not <u>try making your profile public</u> to connect to more people?

Users offline:

tokyo--drifter
Last online:
5 days

daddycool-007
Last online:
26 days

Rowan
Last online:
26 days

destroy_roy
Last online:
28 days

1mp0ssibledream
Last online:
30 days

WesleyCycles67
Last online:
96 days

Connect to a channel to start watching.

No one's online. And that doesn't fill me with the sinking feeling it did before, because I'm not looking to escape into something else today.

My mouse hovers over the 'go public' link. Before, I used to think of this place as being filled with the deep unknown and a rocky seabed waiting at the bottom.

But I suppose that I'm an unknown, too. I lurk inside walls like an eel lying in wait. And I wonder if it's time for people to discover that I exist.

I take a deep breath. I click.

The screen dissolves into a circle that spins and pulses and throws me through it like a portal and I wonder – I wonder – if I have the spoons for this.

Spoon count = 7ish

It's enough, I think.

The screen changes to a tapestry of windows, each one an eye into a different world. And it looks almost exactly like my own private Screen Cast, but wider – with too many live eyes open to count. Some of the worlds are outside – running, roaring, searching, climbing – and they aren't like mine at all. They're surface worlds. And I think I might want to reach up and take one of those as my own, but not yet. Not now.

I look around at the other worlds and they are dark tunnels tumbling into nothingness – and I don't think I want them, either.

But in between. Inside a black panel that flits and twitches and changes as I look at it. Are people. Typing.

Welcome to Stream Cast Public

Search by hashtag to find your people.
You are now viewing the Main Chatroom.

otterish767: welcome to the party, Alice.
teemo: Alice!
x_julie_x: hello hello!
CaB1n-: stream in the sewers – lmfao ☺
squisheroo: has anyone seen Dave?

The messages come and come and they're talking, fast. Some of them welcoming me into their world. But I don't know what to say or how to exist here, or even if I really belong.

At the top of the screen, it says I should search by hashtag to find my people. But who are they?

First I try searching for #sea and #ocean, but nothing but old links and images pop up. I try #painting, #goldfish,

#familylife – but none of them seems like me, and I can feel my energy dropping in spoons.

And then I type that.

#spoons.

spoonie-girl: 2 hours and 300 #spoons later, I actually have make-up on.
>**barefacebear:** @spoonie-girl #spoonielife
>**0_0:** @spoonie-girl feeling this today
>**8jackson8:** @spoonie-girl save some #spoons for leaving the house, bro!

Spoons. *Spoons.*

And these people aren't talking about them like they belong in a cutlery drawer. They're counting them. Using them. Saving them.

I click on the hashtag #spoonielife, and the other chatter dissolves.

#spoonielife

Search by hashtag to find your people.
You are now viewing the chatroom #spoonielife.

barefacebear: bad pain day today >_< #spoonielife
>**0_0:** @barefacebear I'm with you
>**spoonie-girl:** @barefacebear This was me last week, but now I'm baking cookies. CAKE IS WAITING.
>**barefacebear:** @spoonie-girl this is keeping me going rn

My fingers are shaking.

I've read about other people counting spoons when I've been researching online, but the posts always felt impossibly far from me. Other people with Illnesses like mine were like the Loch Ness monster – something you read about, but never really see. Because how could I, when I'm bound to my bed and they're bound to theirs?

I click on the names of each of the people I see talking and read their profiles. Listed on each of their accounts are hashtags about spoons, or diagnoses I've had before, too, or thoughts I've had that have never quite surfaced.

I reach out my fingers.

Are there any live streams about us? #spoonielife

I barely have to wait a moment.

>**barefacebear:** @Alice well volunteered.
>**8jackson8:** @Alice nope!
>**0_0:** @Alice please make this happen.

I'm breathing too heavily, so I snap my laptop shut and stare around at my walls.

These people. These people are in the in-between with me. They count spoons. They drift.

And – like me – they exist.

81

Alice and Rowan

I'm just dozing off when I hear the doorbell go downstairs. I shake the sleep from my eyes and listen.

Mum, walking towards the door. Her hand on the door handle. The creak of the hinges.

'Rowan! Finally come for your review session, have you?'

'Um, yeah, sorry about – Is it okay if –?'

'I'm only kidding. Come in, come in. She's been looking forward to seeing you.'

I die a little bit as I hear the shuffle of him taking off his shoes and I try to tidy my fringe and wipe my face without a mirror.

'So I'll just go up, shall I?'

'You know where it is,' Mum says.

And then footsteps. His footsteps. Coming up to my room. And even though I know that he must have been here before to paint the walls, him being in my room feels big.

The footsteps stop. There's a pause. A breath.

> *She's in there.*
> *Behind that door.*
> *And I don't know what I'm going to see.*

What
DAMAGE
she did
just to help me.
I knock quietly.

'Come in!'

My voice squeaks and then he's coming into the room and he's here. Right in front of me. And I have enough spoons to see now how tall he is. How his hair sits on his shoulders, finger-combed and mahogany brown. The way his clothes fit loosely on him, how he holds himself awkwardly to the side, and the way he plays with the cords of his hoodie as he looks at me, too, and sees me, in this bed.

Me. Alice.

It's Alice.
Her eyes are open and
WIDE,
gulping me in.
And I kind of want to
hide away.
But then I also want to
gulp her in right back.
'Um . . . hi.'

I smile and he smiles back and something inside me flips.

There's a beat of silence and panic hiccups in my chest, making my hand lift up of its own accord and stretch over to him.

338

'Hello,' I say in a mock-serious voice. 'I'm Alice. Pleased to meet you, sir.'

> *She bites her lip.*
> *'Alice,' I smile.*
> *I stride forward,*
> *take her hand in mine.*
> *Shake it.*
> *'Rowan.'*

He looks at me. Not at the strange mechanical bed, or the fact I'm lying in it while he's standing, but at Me. Into my eyes. Deep down inside.

'Sit,' I say, moving my leg a little.

> *I feel a wave of panic because*
> *I'm sitting on her BED.*
> *And I'm so busy thinking about what that means,*
> *I forget to let go of her hand*
> *So we're frozen, mid-shake.*

We look at each other and laugh – our hands held together between us like we're afraid to let go.

Instead, I twist my hand out of his – spinning my skin against his until our palms are flat against each other, joined in the middle.

> *I suck in a breath as she*
> *looks at me.*

'Sort of feels a bit
impossible,
this, doesn't it?
Like I already know you.'

I bite my lip. 'You do know me.'

His hands are on my hands and I can feel his skin and it's making my heart beat out of my chest.

'You've been okay?' I squeak.

I know what she's asking.
She's asking about the
last time she saw me.
When nothing was okay.
I swallow.
'I did what you said.
I called Dad.
Told him what's been going on.'

'Oh,' I say, hooking my fingers round his. 'And?'

Her eyes are like oceans.
And telling her is harder
than I thought it would be.
For a girl
I've only really met
once.

'What did he say?'

I grip his hand. Pull myself forward slightly towards him, so I can smell the mint on his breath.

> *I look at her.*
> *Take a breath.*
> *'He was pretty upset.*
> *I thought he'd be mad at me for not telling him*
> *about Mam leaving,*
> *but he was more angry with himself.*
> *So he came up with this idea*
> *for Jonah and me to stay together.*
> *For me to get some*
> *help*
> *looking after him . . .'*
> *Her eyes.*
> *Her eyes.*

He looks afraid, but I don't know why. I shake him.

'But this is great news! So great, Rowan. You can go to art school. You can –'

> *I clear my throat.*
> *'He says he's got room for Jonah and me.*
> *At his.'*

'But . . .' I still don't know why it looks like he's breaking.

He takes his other hand and sandwiches mine between his.

> *'His. In . . .*

341

And – oh. I remember now.

My gut wrenches like I'm falling.

I want to push him away. I want to cling on to him. I want to rip and scream and dance and shout up to the sky that I don't want him to go. Not there. Not that far away. Not when I've finally got him here with me, Living inside my own lines.

He looks at me and I can feel all of the same words breaking inside of him like waves and –

And I don't think.

For once – for once – I just listen to my body.

I grab his collar –

Push myself forward –

And –

Lips.
Her lips.
Her lips are on mine and
she's kissing me.
And it's unexpected.
And sudden.
But . . .

He kisses me back.

And it feels like we're hurtling towards something huge. Like we're drowning. Like we're falling *down down down*.

Like anything – anything – is possible.

I pull her towards me
and there's something
quick.
Hungry.
And her hands are in my hair.
And my hands are wrapped round her.
And we're sinking into something that could be
something.
Really something.
But . . .

I pull my head away, but we keep our hands together.

'You're going to live in Australia.'

I could stay for her.
I could keep my stupid job at the golf.
I could try.
'I don't have to go,
you know.'

I spit out an impossible smile and our foreheads meet in the middle.

'Yes, you do.' My heart. Aches.

'But – what about you?'
I squeeze her hands.

I crack a laugh. Pull back. Look at him worrying about me. And I use a spoon to lift my thumb and iron out that crease above his eyes.

'Don't you know? All sorts of adventures can be had from a bed, Rowan.'

I nod.
'I'll stream for you
from Australia.
I'll learn how to dive.
I'll −'

I run my finger along the edge of his jaw. My body is screaming at me to shut up talking and run my lips along his lines instead.

But.

But.

'You'll do whatever you want to do,' I whisper. 'You don't need me to tell you what to do.'

His frown lines are back, so I let go of his hands and pull my arms out − wide − like I'm flying.

'I met you. I *kissed* you. And I did all of that without leaving my bed. And if I can do *that* . . .'

She leans close to me
and I wonder if
she's going to kiss me again.

'Imagine what else I can do.'

I swallow.
Our lips dance centimetres apart.
'I've got tomorrow.
One day before I leave.
Just – can we just forget for one day
that I'm leaving
and you're Ill?
Just for one day,
can't we just Live?'

I hold the cuffs of his sleeves.

Forgetting sounds magnificent. But I know enough about fog to know what's left when it's lifted.

'You're leaving,' I whisper. 'I'm Ill.'

He goes to turn away from me and I reach out to hold him back, my fingers brushing through his hair.

'But that doesn't mean we can't Live.'

And seeing her
looking at me like that.
I've never felt more alive.

82

Alice

'Just one day?!' Cecelia says, stuffing her face into a pillow. 'I don't know if that's romantic or just awful.'

I sigh, burying my face in my hands. I tried to rest as much as I could last night, but Rowan's visit is churning inside me, dredging up waves of elation, pain and something else that feels somewhere in between. 'I know, I know.' I poke her cheek. 'But you brought it, yes?'

She slides her face to the side and nods. 'Yeah. But honestly, Alice, if this is some weird sex thing, my mum is gonna flip –'

I flick her. 'Don't. Make. It. Weird.'

She scoots off the bed, laughing. 'Okay, okay. So what do you want me to do?'

Directing her, Mum and Dad from my bed is difficult. I want to march about and check they're doing everything properly, or break up the arguments I can hear coming from along the landing – but I can't. I need every last spoon I can get for today.

Still, though, I hear smashing and shouting, and Dad keeps popping his head round the door and yelling things like, 'Have you seen the plunger?' and, 'Don't worry, that sounded expensive, but nothing in our house really is.'

By midday, my heart is hammering. And Dad comes into my room, drying his hands on a towel and kneeling by my bed.

'You ready, kiddo?' I glare at him and he smiles. 'Not so "kiddo" today, eh? Ladyo?'

'Shut up,' I say, grabbing hold of his neck and taking a deep breath. 'I'm ready, though. I think.'

'Well, too late now.'

He hoists me up, groaning as he carries me out of the door and into the spare room, where Cecelia and Mum are jiggling on the spot.

Only it's not the spare room any more. It's not even a green-screen room. It's the *beach*.

The edges of bright blue tarpaulin poke up from the sides of a floor filled with pebbles and sand, with plastic buckets and spades and even a windbreaker propped up round a sunlounger. Dangling from string from the ceiling are rubber gulls, and playing from speakers in the corner is the sound of them squawking over the swish of the waves.

And then there's the sea. Not on the carpet – because even the very best tarpaulin isn't good enough to stop that being a bad idea. It's –

'Mum's home birthing pool, as requested,' Cecelia says. '*Don't* tell her that we stole it, though, whatever you do. She's got a woman fit to burst any day now who's booked it, so you better hope to God that she doesn't go into labour tonight. Midwife or not – Mum will actually un-birth me if she finds out.'

Mum shakes her head. '"Un-birth"?'

347

'Murder, kill, decapitate – just trying to keep the mood beachy,' she mumbles.

Dad carries me over to the pool and I stare into the water – clear and warm like an exotic sea.

'This does get cleaned between births, doesn't it?' I ask, poking my finger in.

Cecelia rolls her eyes. 'How clean do you think the sea is, Al?'

And she does have a point there.

Dad lays me down on the sunlounger in the middle of the room and I look up at a light bulb that could very well be a real sun.

'Wait,' Mum says, leaning over and popping my sunglasses on me.

'Wait,' Dad says, passing me a bottle of factor-thirty suncream.

I laugh. 'For a light bulb?'

'Alice!' Cecelia says. 'That is the *sun*. And this is the beach. That is the surprisingly unsalty sea and those are birds and you need suncream.'

I smile at her. And Dad. And Mum. 'Thank you,' I say. 'Really. You think he'll like it?'

Just as I say that, the doorbell goes and Cecelia jumps.

Mum rubs her hands together. 'Well, let's find out, shall we?'

Mum and Dad scurry off, but Cecelia leans down, putting her hand over my mouth to stop me hyperventilating.

'Shut up,' she says as I try to speak under her hand. 'No – shhh! You look hot. This room is amazing. And that door –' she points behind her – 'that door is staying CLOSED.'

I lick her hand and she takes it away, grimacing.

'But Mum and Dad –'

She shakes her finger. 'You just leave them to me.'

She has a look in her eye I don't entirely like, but there's no time to say anything, because there – standing at the door and smiling widely at the pool and the fake birds and the sunloungers – is Rowan. And he's here to see me.

I take my sunglasses off.

Cecelia stands up and smacks him over the shoulder.

'You kids have fun,' she says, closing the door behind her with a wink.

83

Alice and Rowan

And now I am locked inside my own small world with Rowan.

> *I smile, looking around*
> *at the pebble floor and the*
> *giant bath in the corner.*
> *'Did you do all this?'*

I shake my head, pointing at myself reclining on the sunlounger.
  'Lugging a beach up here is perhaps a little out of my league.'

> *Shit.*
> *I walk over to her and stop short*
> *so I'm just staring down at her.*
> *'Sorry, I didn't mean . . .*
> *that was a stupid thing to say.'*

'No, it wasn't – I knew what you meant. It was my idea, yes. I know it's not a real beach, but it's . . .'

> *'Better,' I say,*
> *looking at the closed door.*

I smile. 'I think so, too.'

He dithers from foot to foot and I tug on the bottom of his jeans. 'Well, sit down, then. There's a lounger for you, too.'

> *'Um – yeah, okay,' I say.*
> *I take my shoes and hoodie off*
> *and lie down next to her,*
> *our fingers almost touching.*

For a moment, we just lie there, looking up at the swirl of the ceiling and the gulls dancing from strings, listening to Rowan's shallow breaths slowly rolling in time to the wave noises coming from the speakers.

> *I should probably say something.*
> *Or maybe I should just*
> *hold her.*
> *Kiss her while I still can.*
> *I sneak a glance at her and*
> *she's smiling.*
> *Looking up at the ceiling like*
> *it really is the sky.*
> *And she looks so completely –*
> *Alice.*
> *My hand reaches over*
> *the edge of my sunlounger.*

I look down and see his hand inching across the divide between us, but not quite daring to go all the way.

My chest feels heavy and light all at once, like I've swallowed an iron cloud.

I flick my eyes to his and he's looking at me. Lips parted, eyes almost afraid.

Rowan.

I unwind my own hand and reach out.

> *Our fingertips touch.*
> *So lightly, they might not even*
> *be touching at all.*
> *She touches each of her fingers*
> *to mine.*
> *I run my fingerprints*
> *into her palm.*

The waves are steady, but I'm not.

I look at him and he smiles. And it's an impossible smile – like he's stumbled across some rare treasure buried under the floorboards of his living room.

I turn on my lounger to face him, and he does the same, so I'm seeing him from my own angle – in front of me and lying down as the world swirls ahead.

> *Her fringe falls into her eyes*
> *and I use my other hand to*
> *brush it away.*

His eyes dart to my lips and my stomach flips.
'Are you packed for your flight tomorrow?'

> I drop my hand
> like the plane just smashed through the window.
> 'Sort of. Not much to pack.'

'What's your dad's place like? Is Jonah excited?'

> She doesn't take her hand out of mine.
> 'I've not seen it, but
> Dad says it's not far from the beach.
> It has a garden, too.
> We've never had a garden.
> Jonah's a bit gutted about
> leaving his friends, but
> he'll be all right once he gets there.'

I clear my throat. 'How about your friends? Charlie and Fran?'

> I nod.
> 'Yeah, they've been good, actually.
> Since they found out about Mam,
> they've been round a lot,
> helping babysit while
> I pack.
> Makes me wish I'd just
> told them ages ago.

I'll miss them when I go.
Sounds like they'll be all right, though.
They're a bit obsessed with your friend Cecelia.'

I keep my fingers skating on his palm.
'Have you heard from your mum?'

I swallow.
Focus on her hand
in my hand.
'The social tracked her down.
She's been just
ten miles away
all this time, as it goes.
Holed up with
some guy.'

His grip gets tighter.

'We've been given a case worker, though –
Alan.
He's been helping me
work through some stuff.
Like –
I always felt as if what happened was
my fault.
And I still sort of feel that.
But I know more now. That
she's ill, too – my mam.

Not ill like you're Ill or anything, but –
she needs help.'

He frowns like he's trying to force the words into bricks to throw out.

'Help I couldn't have given her.'
I rub my face.

I squeeze his hand back.

'Jonah's lucky to have you. I wish I had a brother like you looking out for me.'

I think of our kiss and
raise an eyebrow at her.
She splits the air
with a laugh.

'You know what I mean.'

She smiles at me, wide.
I bring our hands up to my lips.

He kisses each one of my fingers and my body is screaming at me to leap up and over to him.

I swallow. 'What about –'

'Want to go in the sea?'
I say through her fingers.

My heart thrums and I turn to look at the pool Cecelia brought, sitting on the floor like a beached whale.

'Did you bring your swimming trunks?'

> *I laugh.*
> *'Like that's ever stopped me*
> *throwing myself into the sea.'*
> *I remember the cold in my bones*
> *from last time and*
> *wonder if it's such a good idea*
> *after all.*
> *But the wave noises are like a clock*
> *ticking down the minutes I have left with her.*
> *And I don't want to waste one more second*
> *with questions.*

He drops my hand and gets up.

For a moment, he just sits staring at me, panic shortening his breaths until he smiles.

He keeps his dark-stone eyes on mine as he reaches back – grabs his T-shirt from behind his neck and –

pulls it up and over his head.

And under it I see a chest like a rippled seabed.

Skin smooth like stone.

Hips that curve and disappear under his trousers.

He stands up.

> *She looks at every centimetre of me.*
> *I bend down to her,*

wrapping my arms under her arms and legs
so our faces are centimetres apart.
'This okay?' I ask.

I hold his neck, tight.

'This is okay,' I say.

He picks me up, holds me to his body and I can feel his bare skin on my skin like we're both electric.

He walks me over to the sea, where the noise of the waves is louder, and, for a moment, he just holds me over the water.

'Um – you're still in your clothes.
Did you want to . . . ?'

But I don't. I don't want to pause and stop and think for one more minute.

I look down at the water and back up at him and I smile.

'Throw me. Throw me in.'

I laugh.
'What?'
I look at the door.

I lean in close to him, so our noses are almost touching.

'Throw me.'

She looks at me
like a dare.

357

*She flutters in my hand and
I let her fly.*

And suddenly – water.

It isn't like a bath. The sides are a whole stroke away, and so, for a moment, my head goes under the water and I lose my sense of who I was and who I am and everything.

And there are bubbles and a glug of water pulling at my ankles and wrists as I flap them, and my feet hit the bottom, so I tuck them up and I'm just

floating.

I'm just here. Home. Underwater.

And I open my eyes and see rippling blue on all sides. And I feel the water fluttering as I wave my fingers through it. And I hold my breath and let it bubble out in thick drops and I spin.

Twirl.

Pirouette.

In here, I'm a dancer. I'm a fish.

I'm home.

I gasp up for air and whoop loud, so the anxious look on Rowan's face disappears.

*I haven't killed her.
She is
Alive.
I take off my trousers
and dive.*

The water jumps and waterfalls as he gets in and I paddle to the side, where a ledge offers me a seat to catch my spoons.

He disappears for a moment and, when he comes back up, he's in front of me – hair slicked back and droplets hanging off his eyelashes.

He smiles wide and shakes himself like a dog.

> *It's nothing like the sea.*
> *Not cold or warm – just clear.*
> *I open my eyes and see Alice.*

He's here and I'm here and he's leaving.

The thought throws me up and under like a huge wave and for a moment I gasp and reach out, hooking my hand across his shoulders to stay afloat.

> *'Hey, hey,' I say,*
> *sweeping towards her,*
> *holding her waist under the water.*

The water between us seems to boil.

I lift my feet off the bottom. Wrap my legs round his.

> *My breath catches.*
> *Her skin on my skin.*
> *I pull her closer.*
> *Pull her wet fringe back from her face.*

We're achingly close.

I smile. He laughs.
And then I kiss him.

> *This. This.*
> *THIS.*
> *This could be everything.*

We kiss and the world spins and swims and melts away, so we're caught in between space and time – where a bedbound girl and a boy bound for a whole other world can find each other.

> *She kisses me like she's trying to fit*
> *a whole lifetime*
> *into each brush of her lips.*
> *'I don't have to go,' I say between them.*
> *'We can work something out.'*

Impossible, beautiful words.
I kiss his cheeks and nose. The curve of his shoulder blade.
'We'd be awful. Like Fran and Charlie.'

> *I laugh and spin her round*
> *so the water tornadoes round us.*
> *'We'd be worse.'*

And I want to say, *Stay.*
Stay here and wrinkle with me.

Take a breath and dive to the bottom. Let's float like this together, in the in-between.

But. Eventually. I come up for air. And paddle back over to the seat on the side.

> She closes her eyes and I can see her counting.
> 'Want to get out?'

No, no, I don't ever want to.

I nod.

> She's silent as I
> slip myself up and out of the water.
> Dry myself quickly on a towel before
> coming back to wrap her up in one.
> She bites her lip and so I
> smile. Make jokes. Spin her round
> so all she can see is sky again.

He lays me back down on the sunlounger and I watch him struggling with the other one.

'What are you doing?' I laugh.

> 'It's too far apart, Alice!'
> I point at the tiny space between the two bars.
> 'Too far.'

I laugh and tug him down to me.

'Well then, share mine.'

I make a space for him and he shimmies on to it and somehow I fit like a piece from a missing puzzle into the crook of his arm.

Her body feels warm as we
drip dry.

And, lying together, we talk.

About Mum and Dad. Cecelia's new climbing club.

We each remember Wesley – his bike and his classes.

I ask him about art school, and he tells me about one he's found in his dad's town – a course entirely on street art. And I watch as his fingers seem to hold invisible paintbrushes as he speaks.

She tells me about
people she's found.
People who watch others live
from cameras strapped to their chests.
Just like her.
'Have you spoken to them?' I ask.

I listen as his words rumble inside his chest.

'Not really. Not yet. I asked if anyone streamed from their bed, you know, as there were so many of them watching. But they said they didn't. And that maybe I should.'

'Now that's a stream
I'd like to watch,' I say.

We talk and talk. And then, slowly, he talks and I listen to his heart beating. Beating.

> *'Alice?' I say.*
> *She doesn't reply and I sit up,*
> *turning so I can see her smiling,*
> *but looking almost the same*
> *as when she slipped away from me*
> *in the playground.*
> *'Shit,' I say. 'Should I call your mum?'*

I shake my head, because that means it's over.
   This.
   And I don't want it to be. I don't.
   I lick my lips. 'I forgot,' I whisper. 'There's a toy. For Jonah . . .'

> *I follow her finger to under the lounger*
> *and find a wind-up dinosaur*
> *from a Happy Meal.*
> *I smile.*
> *'He'll love it,' I say.*
> *Although I already know*
> *I'm keeping it for myself.*

I smile and hold his hand.
   'This has been. Wonderful.'

> *My insides liquefy.*
> *I lean over.*

Kiss her on the head.
'You are. Wonderful.'

We are. Both.

But my words are gone and I know he can see them emptying.

He pulls on his T-shirt. Looks at me for a moment more, all to himself.

And I want to say something to make him keep looking at me like that.

But this was just one
      perfect day
           in a wonderfully imperfect life.

I tell her that
I'm going to make myself into something
worthy of the person
she thinks she sees in me.
That one day
I'll come back.
Or that maybe
she'll come forward.
Or we'll meet in the middle and
create a whole new world.
I tell her everything as I lift her.
Open the door, where her family
are waiting.

The door to the beach opens.

The real world sinks back in. And I look up for just one moment more. At his eyes.

Before I

      let

            them

                 go.

84

Alice

It's nearly time.

Cecelia has curled my hair and burned me with the curlers so much it feels like my ear might never recover. Fran and Charlie have dropped by for the third time this week, this time with one of their purple boiler suits. I almost feel like part of their gang now I'm in uniform.

'You so have the boobs for boiler suits, doesn't she, Charlie?' Fran says, playing with my collar as Charlie keeps his eyes on the ray on the ceiling.

Cecelia laughs and whacks him with her hairbrush. 'Charlie – listen to your girlfriend and compliment Alice's boobs already!'

Charlie slinks off to the door, muttering, 'There are too many girls in this group.' He turns to look at me before he leaves, though. 'Good luck, Alice – you'll be great.'

I smile at him as he knocks into Dad on his way out.

'There are a million people on this platform,' he says. 'Did you know that? A million.'

'Dad,' I sigh, trying to stop the butterflies racing round my stomach. 'You're not helping.'

Cecelia steps back and looks at me. 'I'm worried you look *too* hot now. I mean – you're going to be talking about what it's like to have zero energy and looking like fricking Emma Stone or something? It doesn't make sense.'

I bat Fran's hand away as she tries to mess up my hair again.

'Okay – thank you! That's enough. Out you go, all of you.'

All three of them start talking at once and I give them a look until they turn to follow Charlie downstairs. Dad peeks his head round the door just before he closes it. 'You sure you want to do this, kiddo?'

I take a deep breath. And I nod.

'Knock 'em dead!'

He closes the door and then I'm alone again. Just me, in bed, with my laptop.

I look at the clock and I have two minutes until I said I'd be on.

I've been chatting to the other people who call themselves 'spoonies' all week, trying to prepare for it. And more and more people are joining all the time. Wishing me well. Waiting.

And I know they'd understand if I posted now and said that I couldn't do it. That I don't have the energy today.

But I'd be lying. I do. I've been trying to make sure of it – as much as it's possible to do that in a sea as wild as the Illness.

I open my laptop.

Welcome back to Stream Cast, Alice

Users online:

Rowan
Online for:
1 hour

Rowan is online, which means he's managed to get an Australian SIM card. My mouse hovers over his name and I imagine him unpacking his clothes into a new wardrobe. Looking out at Jonah racing round his new garden.

Ready to step outside again into something new.

My chest aches to click and step through to his world and pretend for one moment that I'm there, with him. But I'm not there. I'm here – Alice. In this room and in this bed.

It's time for the world to know that I'm just as much Alive as anyone.

And it's time for me to know that, too.

I click on the camera icon in the top right. My own face flashes up, caught in a tumbling sea. And I can already see the chat waiting.

You've got this, Alice.
Can't waaaaait.
Omg I need this in my life already.

The clock ticks down. I watch myself panic.

But it's time now. It's time to step back inside those windows. And open one of my own.

I take a deep breath.

I hit the green button.

And I smile into the world watching, live.

'Hello,' I say. 'I am here.'

And now I am Alice.

And I am Alive.

Author's Note

Alice is one of an estimated fifteen million people living with a chronic illness in the UK.*

Some of these illnesses can be diagnosed and treated. Other illnesses – like the one Alice has – are trickier. Little is understood about why they start, how best to treat them, and how they differ from one person to the next. Some people even have to fight to be believed that they have an illness at all.

Not everyone with these illnesses will look like Alice. Some could make it to Cecelia's party, but then be unable to get out of bed the next day. A spoon for Alice might be a conversation, but, for someone else, it could be the walk to school.

These illnesses are invisible and can affect people in different ways – and even the same person in different ways from day to day. Some people fully recover, but others have to find new ways to live around their illness.

* Department of Health (2012). 'Long-term conditions compendium of Information' (3rd edition).

It can be difficult for a heathy person to fully appreciate just how an illness like this can impact all parts of someone's life. But we can listen. We can keep turning up, even when they can't make it out. And if we see someone sitting on a priority seat in a packed train, or using a disabled toilet when they might appear to have infinite spoons, we can realize that – just maybe – they might need it.

This story was inspired by real people's lives – particularly the one I care for in my own home. To find out more, I strongly recommend you watch Jennifer Brea's documentary film *Unrest* on Netflix, read the haunting memoir *A Girl Behind Dark Glasses* by Jessica Taylor-Bearman, or speak to your friends who have invisible illnesses.

Thank you so much for reading.

Acknowledgements

A huge thank you to my brilliant editor, Carmen McCullough, who championed this idea from the very beginning. Thank you for your tireless support, ideas and for saying 'yes' to my wacky typesetting requests.

Thanks also to Millie Lean for your keen insights, Shreeta Shah, Jane Tait, Jan Bielecki, Naomi Green, Wendy Shakespeare, Michael Bedo, Simon Armstrong and the entire Penguin team – as well as Helen Crawford-White for creating such a beautiful cover.

Thank you to Sallyanne Sweeney along with Samar Hammam and Marc Simonsson for taking this book far and wide with such passion. Sallyanne, I'm not sure what I'd do without you.

This story was inspired by real lives and my eternal gratitude goes to Julie Farrell for your early insight, as well as the inspirational work of Jennifer Brea, Christine Miserandino and Jessica Taylor-Bearman. A huge thanks also to Jessi Parrott and Inclusive Minds, whose words on this draft made me ugly-cry.

Shout-outs as ever go to my wonderful friends Harriet Venn, Kathryn Davies and Anna Raby, as well as my Brighton ladies, Bumble girls and the team at Jericho Writers (past and present). Thank you to Pippa Lewis for letting me rant about how difficult editing is, and to Ellie Brough for virtual writing Saturdays during lockdown.

This book might never have happened without the daily support and sarcasm from my dark twin, Yasmin Rahman. Katya Balen, who somehow always has the answer (but don't tell her that). Aisha Bushby – the sweetest and most beautiful person I know. Holly Jackson, thank you for waiting with me at Victoria Station. Joseph Elliot, thank you for being you – never stop. Struan Murray, for the Oxford lunches. Lucy Powrie for the cute animal pics, and Sam Copeland for buying me a drink (margarita, thanks!).

My family should win awards for their support on this book and my entire writing career. Mum and Dad – thank you for always being there when I need you. Grandma and Grandad for showing my books to everyone they know. Louise, Jay and Amelia for the yurt in the garden. Thanks also to the Annis family for everything you've done.

Finally, thank you to Dr Ryan Annis for letting me borrow bits of your life for this book. You are, quite literally, an inspiration.

About the author

Sarah Ann Juckes writes books for young people. Her YA debut, *Outside*, was nominated for the Carnegie Medal Award 2020, shortlisted for Mslexia's Children's Novel Award and longlisted for the Bath Novel Award.

She works with writers from all over the world via Jericho Writers and is on the board for Creative Future, a charity supporting under-represented writers. You can often find her hibernating in her writing shed in East Sussex, with her cat.

If you loved **The World Between Us**,
try Sarah Ann Juckes's first novel . . .

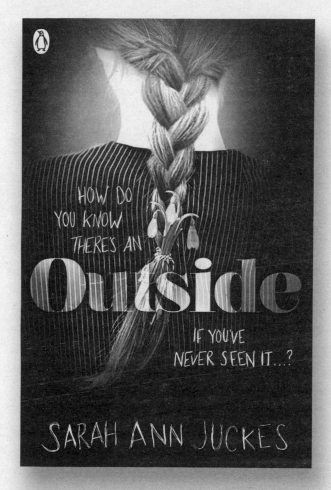

Ele has never been Outside, but she knows
it exists – she just has to prove it.

'Impossible to put down' **C. J. Skuse**